MURDER AT THE BOOK FAIR

When booksellers Molly O'Donnell and Emma Clarke set up at the Antiquarian Book Fair in St. Petersburg, Florida, the last thing they expect to find is a dead body. When respected book dealer Jasper Ross shows interest in Emma's most valuable books, she is jubilant. But then, Jasper is found dead—and Emma's books he borrowed have disappeared.

Then booksellers at the book fair find many of their high-end illustrated volumes missing, then returned—with their color plates cut out. Who would do such a thing? Molly and Emma join forces with Stewart, a transgender print dealer, to get to the bottom of Jasper's murder and the destruction of the books. Their investigation takes them from antique shops in Old Florida coastal towns to the home of Carmen, a flamboyant, small-time drug dealer and former flame of Molly's. Are the book dealers all what they seem? As they investigate, Molly and Emma find their relationship developing into more than friendship. But will they live to enjoy it?

ACKNOWLEDGMENTS

First, we would like to thank members of our two writers' critique groups: Althea Natalga Sumpter, Linda Bell, Valerie Fennell, Brenda Lloyd, Maria Helena Dolan, Victoria Phillips, Ralph Ellis, Mary Stokes, Barbara Brockway, and Priyanka Ozo for their many helpful suggestions. Thanks to Maryann Hopper, Merrill Mushroom, Brenda Lloyd, and Linda Bell for their insightful comments as beta readers. Thanks to Laura Ownbey for editing the manuscript. And to our sister writers at Womonwrites and Outrageous Voices, thank you for your enthusiastic encouragement.

Thanks to Black Opal Books, especially Susan Humphreys, for their confidence in our book and their hard work in turning our manuscript into a finished product.

A special shout-out to Sarah Smith and her team who organize the Florida Antiquarian Book Fair.

And finally, we would like to thank each other for being the best co-writer imaginable.

Libby Ware and Charlene Ball, aka Lily Charles

Other Books by Lily Charles
Murder at the Estate Sale

Murder At The Book Fair

Lily Charles

A Black Opal Books Publication

GENRE: BIBLIOMYSTERY/LGBTQ

This is a work of fiction. Names, places, characters and incidents are either the product of the author's imagination or are used fictitiously, and any resemblance to any actual persons, living or dead, businesses, organizations, events or locales is entirely coincidental. All trademarks, service marks, registered trademarks, and registered service marks are the property of their respective owners and are used herein for identification purposes only. The publisher does not have any control over or assume any responsibility for author or third-party websites or their contents.

DEDICATION

To those of all ages who love children's books

Chapter 1
Her Best Books

Dr. Seuss (Theodore Geisel), And to Think That I Saw It on Mulberry Street, *New York: Vanguard Press, 1937. Illustrations by the author. Pictorial boards with dust jacket. First edition with white shorts on boy.*

Emma stood back, arms crossed, and sighed with satisfaction at her booth in the St. Petersburg, Florida, Coliseum. Clarke's Collectibles looked like a real, inviting bookshop. The teenaged porter had left an hour ago after putting her boxes in the middle of the floor and setting up her collapsible shelves on the three tables that formed a small booth. Emma had proceeded to remove books from the boxes and arrange them on shelves according to category: Illustrated Classics, 20th Century Children's, Newbery Winners (best children's literature for the year), and a small row of books under fifty dollars. She had pondered which of her best or most striking books would go on stands facing forward. She settled on three illustrated classics with covers by Howard Pyle, Jessie Willcox Smith, and Arthur Rackham, and her most beautiful book, a vellum-covered limited edition of *East of the Sun and West of the Moon,* signed by Kay Nielsen, the famous Danish artist, in a slip case, prominently displayed. She had paid $5,000 for it and was selling it for $22,000. She'd hesitated to spend so much, but her friend Molly O'Donnell had urged her to buy it. Her second most valuable was a signed first edition of Dr. Seuss's first book, *And to Think That I Saw It on Mulberry Street.*

Emma's last book fair was on Labor Day Weekend in Atlanta, her hometown, and she had done so badly that she wondered if she should even stay in the book business. However, she had bought many books for her stock. When she complained about the fair to some booksellers, Eliot, one of the veteran dealers, said in a consoling voice, "Sometimes you just have to buy your way out of a book fair." Mignon Chambray, a Miami bookseller who sold children's books, said, "What you should do is add the amount that you spent on books plus the amount from sales to know how much you made."

Emma bristled at her tone, although if she did add in her purchases, she did well.

"And sometimes you have to drink your way out." Jay Hardy grinned. Jay was one of the Atlanta booksellers. He had seemed cocky and boastful at first, but Emma had come to like him.

After the Atlanta book fair, before she even had a chance to catalog her newest acquisitions, her father had a heart attack, and she went to North Carolina to take care of him. In March he had another that was fatal. As his executor, she stayed long enough to settle the estate, and then she came back to Atlanta in time to get ready for the Florida show. She had to focus on deciding what to take to St. Pete, getting her books in proper order, cataloging and pricing new ones, making discreet repairs, slipping on mylar covers, and putting them in sturdy boxes. All in the week between arriving home and heading to St. Petersburg.

Emma hit the road in her Volvo station wagon, packed

to bursting with boxes of books and supplies including an old leather pouch to hold cash. After spending the night with some friends in Gainesville, she drove the rest of the way to St. Petersburg on Thursday afternoon.

She had felt excited when she approached the long bridge that connected St. Pete to the mainland. She gazed with pleasure at the blue water under her and the blue sky above as the bridge rose and then leveled off, and the water stretched out in shades of green and blue on either side. She heaved a sigh of satisfaction as the bridge sloped down, and she was on the ground in St. Pete.

❧❦❧

Now, in the Coliseum, she looked forward to seeing her friend Molly's loping stride and wide smile over a T-shirt with some kind of book-related or political slogan and felt disappointed that Friday afternoon had arrived already without Molly appearing. Emma and Molly had become friends the previous year when the two of them, in searching for a missing sixteenth century manuscript, had found themselves investigating a murder that dropped them into a coven that practiced black magic.

Their friendship had gradually become something more, yet neither of them was ready to carry it into relationship territory. They both treasured their solitude and independence. She and Molly had gotten together a few times to talk books over coffee, drinks, or an occasional meal. Their friendship had become comfortable to Emma as soon as she was sure it would remain as it was for the time being. She hoped that maybe at some point it would become more, and occasionally she found herself having dreams that featured Molly, but she was in no hurry. She counted on Molly to make the first gesture, and maybe that was a mistake.

At first, she and Molly had emailed and called each

other often, but during the seven months she had been away from Atlanta, the calls and emails had become less frequent. When they first saw each other, a kind of awkwardness was between them. The intimacy that had seemed promising failed to materialize. Molly seemed busier than ever.

They had planned to meet up on Thursday evening for a burger and craft beer at the pub in Molly's hotel, the Flying Dutchman. Emma had been disappointed to get a call after ten on Thursday from Molly saying that she had just arrived. But Emma, hungry and tired of waiting for Molly, had gone to the Indian restaurant near her own motel. She suggested they go out Friday instead, after opening night of the book fair. After chatting a few minutes, Emma had said good night and got into bed with a book.

Emma wiped her forehead and neck with a bandana—setting up in the Florida heat and humidity was sweaty work—and looked around at the booths on her row, some conventionally named like Smith's Old Books, Carter's Antiquarian Books, and Mignon Chambray, Bookseller. Some had more imaginative names such as Magical Voyages, On the Road to Mandalay, and Fine Books and Golden Treasures. She looked up at the arching ceiling of the Art Deco building. Pastel turquoise and light sand-colored arcs, balconies, and walls swung up and out of sight all around her. She loved this building and the Florida Antiquarian Book Fair that took place here each spring. Posters in the lobby recalled momentous past days: of concerts by jazz greats, galas celebrating political wins, and elegant ballroom dances with tuxedos, sweeping satin ball gowns, and elbow-length gloves. A few stills from the movie *Cocoon* of a ballroom dance scene that had been filmed in the Coliseum were included.

Outside, the building carried on the turquoise and sand-colored theme, surrounded by bougainvillea, mimosas, and sable palms. A marquee announced tea dances each Thursday.

Emma was pleased with her booth's location—second from the end of its row between the snack bar and the bathrooms. *Everyone must pass by here at least once,* she thought.

Two booths down she saw Jasper Ross, stooped and lanky, wearing rumpled khaki pants and a tan windbreaker, bending over at the waist to peer inside a glass case. She wondered why he was wearing a windbreaker since it was so warm in the Coliseum. She crossed her fingers behind her back. Her last Florida show had been successful, largely thanks to Jasper. He and his wife Eileen were mainstays in the children's book world. In their seventies, they had set up at the Florida fair for decades.

Emma went inside her booth, ready to show Jasper what she'd brought. She'd priced *East of the Sun* low enough so that a dealer could make money, but she would still make a nice profit. Nice, heck! That one sale would make her show!

"Oh, you're here again." He frowned as though trying to remember who she was.

Emma looked up at Jasper and smiled. "Yes, I am. Hoping this will be my permanent spot." He stared at her, tapping his chin. She held out her hand. "Emma."

"Emma, of course." A genial smile replaced the frown. "Your name was on the tip of my brain." He enveloped her hand in his large one that felt dry and hard, almost like a worn parchment cover. "Anything interesting?"

She lifted her prize, the *East of the Sun,* white vellum with gilt lettering. "This is the limited edition signed by Nielsen."

"Oh my," he breathed and gingerly reached for it. She let it go with some reluctance. He took it lightly and turned to the page stating 500 limited edition copies, number 296, with its tiny, scrawled signature.

"And look at the title page—he signed it again."

He gasped. "Signed twice?! I've sold many editions of *East of the Sun*, but I've never even seen this one. I can't wait for Eileen to see it. Illustrated fairy tales and fables are her bailiwick." He flipped to the bookmark on which she had written her price. "Quite reasonable, my dear." He paged through the volume, looking at a few illustrations, and then laid the book down on her table. "What else?"

Emma handed him a large, flat book. "First edition signed *And to Think That I Saw it on Mulberry Street*."

"Ah." He tapped the dust jacket. "White shorts," he said with a satisfied smile. "You know the later editions all had blue shorts on the boy." He peered at the tears in the dust jacket's spine and turned to the bookmark where Emma's price, $10,000, was written. "Not bad. Start a pile for me, will you?"

"Sure." Was she going to sell her top items before the fair opened? She sure hoped so.

Jasper didn't select everything she showed him, but he stacked up five books: *The Little Prince*; *Alice in Wonderland*, illustrated by Ralph Steadman; *A Child's Garden of Verses*, illustrated by Jessie Willcox Smith; *And to Think That I Saw It on Mulberry Street*; and *East of the Sun*. Every so often, he craned his head around and looked up and down the aisle. "Of all the dumb things, I left my phone in the booth, so I can't call Eileen. I want her opinion on the *East*. I hope she'll come this way." He sat in Emma's extra chair and flipped through his book choices. Emma set up her receipt book, hooked up the credit card reader, and lined up pencils and pens on her little folding table.

After a while, Jasper said in a puzzled voice, "I thought she would be here by now. I know she wants to see what you have, too." He cleared his throat. "Oh, I just remembered that she sprained her ankle and is having trouble walking around. Do you mind terribly if I carry these over to show her?" He rolled his eyes. "Eileen won't let me buy anything without her approval. She's the boss."

Emma thought, *He's just now remembering that she sprained her ankle?* She felt uneasy letting him take the books without buying them, but Molly said they'd been selling at the Florida Book Fair for decades.

Jasper hoisted the books onto one bony hip and wandered away.

Chapter 2
Around the Corner

Robert Louis Stevenson, A Child's Garden of Verses, *London: John Lane, The Bodley Head, 1896. Illustrated by Charles Robinson. First British illustrated edition. Green cloth with gilt titles and decoration on spine. Rear board has gilt design, all page edges are gilt. Black and white text illustrations by Robinson. A children's classic, first published under the name "Penny Whistles."*

Molly exited the bathroom and headed toward Emma's booth. To her delight, Emma was there. She wore a red tank top with wet marks around her upper chest and armholes. Her black, gray-streaked hair was pulled back with an elastic band, and she wore no makeup. Molly's heart gave a little skip.

Emma jumped out of her chair as soon as she saw Molly. "Hey!" she said. They hugged, both of them sweaty and sticky.

Molly said, "Sorry I got in so late last night. I was really looking forward to having a beer and a burger with you."

"Me too. But, hey, you'll never believe it—I just sold some of my best stuff: the *Mulberry Street, Alice* with the Steadman illustrations, *A Child's Garden of Verses* with

Jessie Willcox Smith's illustrations, and—tah dah! —*East of the Sun*." She threw out her arms dramatically.

"Way to go!" Molly raised her palm for a high-five, and Emma cautiously slapped it. "Who'd you sell your books to?"

"Jasper Ross. He hasn't paid yet because he has to get Eileen's approval."

"So, I guess you don't regret buying all those high-end books after all."

"No! Only thing is—he's been gone with the books for over an hour."

"Maybe another dealer is shopping in their booth, and he can't leave."

"Yeah, I guess. He said Eileen sprained her ankle. But he only said that after looking for her up and down the aisle, as though he had just remembered."

Molly shrugged. "Probably getting a tad forgetful. I'll swing by their booth and let you know what's up—unless you'd like to go too and check out their books."

"Okay. Are you set up?"

"Pretty much. I just need to straighten out my ephemera. I was up late Wednesday night pricing some *Mattachine Reviews*." In addition to occult/esoteric, one of Molly's specialties was LGBTQ+.

They lingered over some booths, Molly stopping to examine some oversized posters of early twentieth-century circuses. "Here's an ad with the Turtle Boy," she murmured to Emma.

Across the aisle, Emma was drawn to a display of the Sunbonnet Babies books, first-grade readers from the 1930s featuring small children in profile wearing sunbonnets that hid their faces. Molly looked up: the booth was Mignon Chambray's.

Mignon glanced up from the *Southern Living* magazine she was reading. She wore jeans and a low-necked knit blouse. Her blonde hair fell in waves to her shoulders.

"Oh, hello," she said. "Feel free to look around, but I'm going back to the hotel and shower."

"Molly," Emma said, "Look at this *Peter Rabbit.*" She was looking at a book in Mignon's case.

Mignon murmured, "It's the first edition, the one she self-published in 1901. If you'd like to look at it, I'll unlock the case." Mignon's voice seemed to imply that she was ready to leave.

"That's all right," Emma said. "We're on our way to Ross Books."

When they reached Ross Books, Eileen was sitting with her swollen ankle propped up on a chair. The two front wings of her chin-length silver hair hung straight, held back from her face by two silver barrettes. Her long denim skirt had been gathered up to her knees. The booth looked about half set up, with boxes full of books still in the middle of the floor between the tables.

Emma said, "Hi, Eileen. I'm sorry about your ankle. Jasper told me."

"Oh, you saw him? When?"

"About two hours ago. He was going to show you some books, including my signed copy of *East of the Sun.*"

Eileen's eyes lit up. "Signed?"

"Yes, the limited edition signed twice by Kay Nielsen!"

"What other books?"

Emma told her.

"That fool. He's probably chatting with everyone. He wandered off before he finished setting up the booth."

"Oh, okay. I was a little worried."

Eileen shifted in her seat and winced. "To tell you the truth, I'm anxious about him. He's gotten so forgetful lately. I told him this was going to be our last show. Whenever we travel, he gets nervous being in unfamiliar places. But I figured since we've been coming here for twenty-eight years…" Her voice trailed off as she looked around. "Well, if you see him, tell him I need him."

"Anything we can do for you?" Molly asked.

"If you could, see if the snack bar can give you some ice." She lifted a red rubber water bottle. "All of mine melted. It's still cool, but not cold enough to keep the swelling down."

"Sure thing." Molly picked up the water bottle.

"I'll look around for Jasper," Emma said.

"Tell that old coot to get his ass over here!" Eileen called after her.

Chapter 3
Where's Jasper?

Tolkien, J. R. R., The Hobbit or There and Back Again, *London: George Allen and Unwin, 1937. First edition. Green cloth with dark blue titles and illustration. Pictorial dust jacket. Illustrated by the author with 4 color plates, 9 black and white full-page plates, and double page map illustrations front and rear.*

Emma didn't experience her usual pleasure of wandering around the Coliseum because she couldn't concentrate on both looking at books and talking with people. At her first book fair, she'd been awed by the hundred-plus booths that lined the aisles as she walked up and down them, browsing at will. Now she found herself recognizing and greeting booksellers who had become friends. She'd met a number of people she was glad to see and chat with. But now this was her third book fair, and the second time she'd set up in St. Pete, and she wasn't able to stroll in happy anonymity anymore. Moreover, she couldn't stop worrying that Jasper had probably mislaid her best books in someone else's booth.

She dropped by Mountain Books, run by Dan and Carol Underwood, a couple who lived in north Georgia and specialized in American and Southern history and Black Americana. Dan looked up, wrinkling his long, thin face into a smile.

"Hi, Dan!" Emma exclaimed. "When did you all get here?"

"We drove down yesterday," Dan answered. "Carol's out shopping for containers to bring the pancakes to the book fair. She's made a special whole-grain recipe this time with apple cinnamon topping." Carol brought something special every year for the Saturday morning Antiquarian Booksellers of Georgia breakfast at ABOG's semi-annual meeting.

Emma shook her head in amazement. "Apple cinnamon topping? That sounds so good."

"She likes to do it," Dan said. "Brings the batter and fruit in our cooler and sets up a hot plate in the motel room. She just realized she needed more containers to bring the food over to the Coliseum."

"I'm impressed," Emma said. "So how have you all been?"

"We went out to Colorado to see our grandkids for their Spring break. Being retired is great." Dan had recently retired from his thirty-year job as an English professor.

"Any new books?" Emma asked.

"I've got a few on Shakespeare," he said. "Look over on that shelf; there's a new one about how the Earl of Oxford really wrote Shakespeare's plays."

"You don't believe that, do you?" Emma was convinced that Shakespeare wrote Shakespeare and scoffed at all the conspiracies.

He shook his head. "All kinds of theories come and go. I say, just read the plays and don't pay any attention to that other stuff."

"Right!" Emma agreed. After a little more Shakespearean chat, she moved on.

Her next stop was Over the Hills and Far Away. Jerry, the owner, a short guy with curly black hair and a salt and pepper mustache, sat rocking back on his chair, seemingly absorbed by a book in his lap. He had a first edition of *The Hobbit* propped up on a stand. Emma picked it up and held it carefully, and when Jerry looked up, she said, "Nice copy."

"Just got it," he said. He placed the book he had been reading, *If I'm Not a Buddhist by Now, I Never Will Be,* face up on his table.

She looked around a little more and said, "Have you seen Jasper Ross?"

"He was here earlier. Like you, he zoomed in on *The Hobbit.*"

"Eileen's worried about him and she has a bum ankle, so I told her I would keep an eye out for him."

"He is getting a little forgetful," Jerry said. "He asked me if I had any *Anne of Green Gables*, and I pointed out the shelf where there were several. He muttered, 'Montgomery, of course.'"

"Did you notice if he was carrying any books?" Emma glanced around, hoping to find *East of the Sun* or *Mulberry Street* lying on one of Jerry's tables.

"I don't remember." Jerry shook his head.

"I'm just worried because he took five of my books to show Eileen, and she hasn't seen him." She listed the books.

"Wow! A first *Mulberry*? I don't think I've ever seen one. I can see why you're worried. I'll keep an eye out for them. How long ago was he in your booth?"

"A couple of hours." Emma remembered that Jasper had refused a bag because he was supposedly going to his own booth, so he had left carrying the books under his arm. "What time is it?"

"Almost three-thirty."

Emma knew well how time ceased to exist when she was looking at books whether at a bookstore, a library sale, or at one of the book fairs. *He was in my booth around one o'clock*, Emma thought. *Maybe he's found his way to his own booth by now.* She decided to go back to Ross Books. *He probably remembered that Eileen needed him.*

Eileen was still in her chair with her foot up while a young man, one of the porters, was emptying her boxes and shelving the books.

"Have you—?" Eileen said at the same time as Emma said, "Any sign—?"

"You haven't seen him, have you?" Eileen twisted her denim skirt in her hands.

"No. So sorry. I looked for him and asked around, but if anyone had seen him…" Emma's voice trailed off. She didn't think she should mention her missing books; after all, Eileen was worried about her husband. "It was a while ago."

"I'm gonna kill him!" Eileen's eyes glistened. "I never should've agreed to come here. I mean, my ankle being sprained must've been a sign that we were better off at home."

"I'm sure he'll show up. Anybody who's a good friend that he might be with?"

"He has lots of friends here. But he and Antonio Alvarez like to pal around together."

"Excuse me, Ma'am," the porter looked up at Eileen. "Where do these go?" He held up an illustrated copy of *Treasure Island.*

As Eileen directed him to the illustrated classics shelf, Emma decided to go back and check on her booth. Someone might have tried to buy a book while she was away. "I'm going back to my booth now, Eileen. Jasper will show up soon."

Eileen said, "He will. He wouldn't miss the Friday night

opening."

Emma didn't think Eileen's face looked as confident as her words. She was starting to worry herself. She would look up Antonio Alvarez in the book fair directory and check with him after she had a minute to just sit in her own booth and rest before going back to her motel, showering, and changing for the five o'clock opening.

She felt a rush of joy at the sight of her own little mini bookstore, her own cavern of treasures. If only *Mulberry Street* were on the empty stand in the center.

Chapter 4
Opening Night

Mary Mapes Dodge, Hans Brinker or The Silver Skates: A Story of Life in Holland, *New York: James O'Kane, 1866. First edition of the author's best-known children's novel. Blue cloth boards, gilt title to spine, gilt publisher's initials on front board. Four full page illustrations by F. O. C. Darley and Thomas Nast.*

Molly always loved opening night. Kitty's cheerful voice over the microphone announcing, "The Florida Antiquarian Book Fair is now OPEN!" harp music from the mezzanine, and shoppers trickling in—casually dressed Florida residents and tourists in flip-flops, shorts, and sundresses flowed through the aisles, stopping in booths to browse, taking down books and replacing them, and quickly moving on. More well-heeled shoppers also streamed through in loose dresses, pressed chinos, or prim, piped blazers despite the heat. Some looked as though they had come from dinner, others from the beach. Kids pulled parents, and teenagers in clumps pulled one another toward a particular booth. "Hey, look at this!" Youngsters, some reluctant, some rapt, wide eyes darting around.

Twice Kitty's voice came over the loudspeaker asking Jasper Ross to return to his booth. Molly had already slipped over to check with Eileen. He was still missing. Eileen's daughter Melissa and her husband Jim were with her.

Molly stepped back into her own booth, avoiding the browsers, and swept her eyes over her treasures: her Arthur Waite book on Rosicrucianism prominently displayed, its white cover with gilt Celtic cross making an eye-catching display. Her Occult/Esoteric shelves were well populated, thanks to her purchase of an extensive, valuable occult library last year. This was her main specialty, and she was one of the few booksellers who dealt in these books. She looked forward to the young people in black who would huddle over them, whispering and conferring before buying some Theosophist tract or something by Aleister Crowley or Alice Bailey. Once she had sold about a dozen books to a purple-haired, savvy young bookseller with an Orlando shop named Bells, Books, and Black Cats.

On the opposite table stood *Copper Sun* by Countee Cullen with its beautiful Art Deco cover; her stack of issues of *The Crisis*, the NAACP magazine; Abolitionist ephemera; the Mattachine Society's newsletters; and issues of *The Ladder* printed by the Daughters of Bilitis, all protected in plastic sleeves. Maybe that guy from the LGBTQ+ Archives might be interested.

Emma dropped by in her floating cobalt blue tunic over black leggings, topped by a colorful print scarf. Molly smiled to see her fashion-conscious friend. Molly sported tan hemp trousers, a gauzy cotton tunic, a jacket in purples and blues, and purple socks to match.

"Hey!" Molly exclaimed. "How's your book fair going?"

Emma gave an uncertain smile. "A couple of big-time dealers breezed through. But my prize books that I'd hoped might draw them are still missing."

"Bummer!" said Molly.

"But I did sell a nice *Hans Brinker* and that *Back of the North Wind* that I've had for a while. The nostalgia factor always works. How about you?"

"I sold three Abolitionist pamphlets and an 1880s book on Spiritualism. And someone said they would come back tomorrow for another look at the signed Arthur Waite." Molly hesitated. "Say, Emma, are you still up for that beer and burger tonight?" She hoped her face hadn't turned pink, although she felt it grow warm.

"Sure," Emma said.

"All right!" Molly felt a rush of anticipation.

∽∾∽

At nine o'clock, Kitty's ever-cheerful voice came over the loudspeaker announcing, "The Book Fair is CLOSED! We open tomorrow at ten."

As the remaining stragglers drifted out, Molly hurried up to Emma's booth. "Let's go grab that beer!" As Emma glanced up, Molly added, "Or wine." Molly knew that Emma preferred wine and was selective about what kind she got. The bar at The Flying Dutchman had an extensive beer list, so Molly hoped they also had a wine list to Emma's liking.

"Okay, I'm ready." Emma carefully pushed her two chairs into the fourth wall of her booth, indicating that it was closed. She gave the booth another look, a worried frown between her black brows, and patted her shoulder bag. "I didn't do as well as I'd hoped tonight."

"There's always tomorrow," said Molly. "Sometimes I don't sell much of anything the opening night. And you did have a great sale this afternoon."

Emma's worried expression didn't change. "I'm just so

anxious about those books. I had hoped they would get snapped up by one of the big-time dealers. Marge Blumenschein came by, glanced into my booth, and walked on. If *East of the Sun* had been there, I'm sure she would have at least looked at it." Marge Blumenschein was the well-known owner of a Fifth Avenue bookshop.

"You'll get it back," Molly said.

Emma nodded, but her worry line didn't fade. "How about I drive us over to The Dutchman? Then I'll have my car to go to my motel."

"Good idea." Molly had walked from her hotel since it was only a few blocks from the Coliseum.

❧❧

They pulled up in the parking lot behind The Flying Dutchman. The lot was tiny, squeezed in between the old, newly opened, and refurbished brick hotel and the equally old stucco building beside it. Sable palms, palmettos, and vinca growing wild crowded its edges. Its paving stones were cracked and broken. A weak streetlight showed that the little lot looked full.

Molly pointed to a narrow space beside a dumpster. "I think that's a space. I saw Mignon's Prius there earlier."

Emma pulled her station wagon into the narrow space. "Let's hope we can get out," she said as she wrung the steering wheel around and straightened the car.

"What's that by the dumpster?" asked Molly as she got out of the passenger side door.

"I don't know—maybe an old coat?" Emma locked the door and turned toward the back hotel entrance that led to the bar.

"Mmm," Molly muttered. She went over to the dumpster.

"Come on." Emma urged.

"Just a minute."

"What's the matter?" Emma came over to stand beside her.

Molly bent down to look at a light-colored piece of fabric. It looked like the sleeve of a tan windbreaker—with an arm inside.

"Molly, don't." Emma's voice sounded impatient. "Probably a homeless person sleeping. Let's not—"

"I don't think so." Molly bent over the form on the ground. "Look how splayed out he is. People don't sleep like that." She'd seen lots of homeless men in St. Pete, some lying on the ground. But this man looked different.

"Oh, my god!" Molly clapped her hand over her mouth. "It's Jasper!" Then she saw the blood.

Chapter 5

Death by the Dumpster

Antoine St. Exupéry, The Little Prince, *New York: Reynal and Hitchcock, 1943. Illustrated by the author. Signed limited first edition of 525 numbered copies. Small quarto, salmon cloth with pictorial dust jacket*

Even in the dim light, Emma turned her phone's flashlight on. Jasper lay mostly in shadow, sprawled face up. His mouth had fallen partially open. Dried blood covered his chest and had spattered over a mass of weeds edging the parking lot.

Molly dialed 911 while Emma avoided looking at the man she had been talking with about books a few hours ago. *White shorts*, she thought. *Now I'll always associate those shorts on the cover of* Mulberry Street *with Jasper.*

"Yes," Molly was saying into her phone, "the parking lot of the Flying Dutchman. Yes, he appears to be dead." She nodded, said "yes," a few more times and then, "okay, we'll be here." She clicked off her phone and came to stand by Emma.

"The police will be here soon," Molly said.

"I wonder if he had the books with him." Emma circled the dumpster and looked inside an open door, but there was no sign of them. Panic began to spread inside her. "Oh my god, what if he was murdered for my books?"

"Who could do such a thing? I'd better call Eileen."

After Molly called, they stood side by side, heads bowed, not speaking, Molly with hands in her hemp trouser pockets. Emma clutched her shoulder bag. Shadows of palm tree branches moved against the brick wall, lit by a weak streetlight. Emma heard the faint sound of R&B tunes from the hotel bar. The image of her father lying in his coffin passed through her mind.

A police car pulled up. Two doors slammed, and a pair of uniformed officers appeared. They looked around for a moment before focusing on Molly and Emma.

One of the officers asked, "You called 911?"

"Yes, Officer." Molly pointed. "Behind the dumpster."

"I'm Officer Lincoln," the woman said. "This is Officer Valdez." She gestured to her partner, who nodded to them.

"I'm Molly O'Donnell, and this is Emma Clarke," Molly said, extending her hand. The officer ignored her gesture and squatted down beside Jasper's body. After a moment, she looked up and nodded to her fellow officer. "Yeah," she said in a low voice.

"We know who he is," Emma said. She stood with her back to the dumpster while Officer Valdez took down the information about Jasper.

A small car pulled into the lot and stopped. Jasper and Eileen's daughter Melissa, a twenty-something Asian woman with smooth black hair pulled back in a ponytail, leaped out of the driver's seat. Her husband Jim opened the back door to help Eileen out. Eileen hopped, holding up her injured foot and leaning on his arm. She looked down at Jasper's body and then bent over and lightly touched his cheek. "You crazy old man," she murmured. Tears were running down her face, and she wiped her cheeks roughly with her hand. She turned to the officers and said almost inaudibly. "It's my husband, Jasper." She buried her face in Jim's chest. "Please, I can't look at him any longer." She sobbed.

Jim led Eileen to the car, and she sat in the back seat with her leg stretched out. Emma could hear the officers asking her questions.

Eileen said, "Yes, he has a brown wallet."

The police officer nodded. "Does he carry a cell phone?"

"He left it in the booth."

"We'll need to take it. Do you have it with you?"

"I took it home."

"Do you have any idea who could have done this?"

"No," she said quickly. "I don't even know why he was at this hotel. I was afraid something would happen to him. But I thought it would be from dementia. It's all my fault."

"You mean—?" Valdez asked.

"I should've known he wasn't himself enough to do a book fair. I just kept denying that he was as—far gone into dementia as he was." She wiped her eyes. Her voice sounded suddenly clearer. "I always hoped he'd get to die quietly, surrounded by his books—" She abruptly broke off and wiped her nose.

After a few more words, the officers told her she could go. Melissa called Kitty, the book fair manager, and got permission to come to the Coliseum early the next day and dismantle the Ross Books booth before the Saturday show opened.

Molly and Emma asked Eileen if there was anything they could do for her.

"No, I don't need anything right now. Melissa and Jim have got it covered. I don't want to go back to the fair, though. I just couldn't stand to see the looks on the other dealers' faces and hear their offers of comfort." She wiped her eyes. "I feel like Dorothy Parker at her husband's funeral," she said, trying a rough chuckle that threatened to become a sob. "When someone asked her if they could do anything for her, she said, 'Yes, get me a new husband.'"

Molly squeezed her shoulder. "Yeah, no words. I know."

"Ms. O'Donnell?" Officer Lincoln called. "Could you step over here for a minute?" She gestured for Molly to follow her to the other side of the parking lot.

Officer Valdez said to Emma, "So you two ladies found him here?"

"Yes, Officer. Molly saw the light-colored windbreaker next to the dumpster and called me over to see what it was. I was reluctant because I thought it was a sleeping homeless person." She paused. "Actually, I think I might have recognized that tan windbreaker without realizing it. Earlier he came to my booth at the book fair and took some expensive books to show his wife, but he never made it back to his booth."

The officer said, "Please stick around. The detectives will be here shortly."

A car pulled up, and a man and a woman in street clothes got out.

"Detective Paul Rodriguez," the man said, extending his hand. He was middle-aged and brown-skinned with gray, close-cropped hair, and he wore horn-rimmed glasses.

Emma took his hand and introduced herself.

"I'm Detective Greenfield." The young African American woman spoke to Molly.

After giving their story to the detectives, Emma and Molly agreed to stay over in St. Pete so they could be interviewed on Monday.

Emma and Molly were finally sitting in a booth at the Flying Dutchman's bar, their drinks in front of them. Emma was definitely ready for a glass of red wine. She took a swallow of her Argentine Malbec, feeling its warmth spread through her.

Molly sipped from a frosty mug. "Want a taste of my Guinness?"

Emma sipped Molly's beer and grimaced. "Looks like crude oil and tastes like molasses." She pushed the mug back to Molly, who grinned and took a long swallow.

"Poor Jasper and poor Eileen. I can't imagine what she is going through tonight." Emma remembered Eileen's sobbing. "She said it was her fault."

"She was the one who kept Ross Books going for years, I'm sure. Protecting Jasper, not letting people know how far gone he was."

"I just thought he was forgetful. But, come to think of it, it was Eileen who bought all those books from me last year after he pointed them out to her. I told Detective Rodriguez to keep an eye out for my missing books. I gave him a list."

Molly said, "I hope we're not suspects since we're the ones who called the police."

Emma had never seen Molly drink down a beer so fast. "Why do we keep stumbling on dead bodies?" Emma asked.

"Just lucky? Let's hope this is the last one."

Emma gestured for another glass of wine, although it was late.

Molly said, "I'll have another one, too."

Emma said, "I still have to drive back to my motel. And I need to get some sleep and be at the Coliseum by nine in the morning all bright and brisk and ready to sell books." Her heart sank at the thought that her best books were missing. She sipped her wine.

After they finished their drinks, Emma said, "I better go. I'm exhausted."

She opened her arms, and Molly hugged her tight,

whispering, "We'll get through this. We did once before."

Chapter 6
Even at the Book Fair?

Lewis Carroll, Alice in Wonderland, *London: Dobson Books Limited, 1967. Illustrated by Ralph Steadman. White boards with black lettering and design. Black dust jacket with white and gray lettering.*

Molly handed a bag to the man who had just bought two Florida books. "Thanks for your business."

"I hope you have more Florida books next time," he said.

Molly smiled and said nothing. She had been trying to get rid of those Florida books for years. They were pretty books with vintage dust jackets depicting palms, blue skies, water, and people poling flatboats through the Everglades, all in a wash of Deco pastels. But they had sat on her shelves for a decade, and she felt like whooping with joy to see the last of them. She planned to reduce all categories except Occult, LGBTQ+, and ephemera, her best sellers and her own favorites.

❧❧❧

Before the book fair started, the Antiquarian Booksellers of Georgia (ABOG) book dealers had been eating pancakes in the snack area. They had been all abuzz about Jasper's death. Molly and Emma could hardly get their pancakes and Carol's apple-cinnamon topping onto their plates before being inundated with questions when people found out that they had discovered the body.

Jay, as usual, had something smart-alecky to say. "I know book dealers are competitive, but this is ridiculous." He tried to smooth his red hair, but it sprang back as soon as his hand moved.

Harry shook his head. "Don't joke about it, man." A necklace of silver beads hung on his black shirt.

Molly stirred half-n-half into her coffee with a wooden stirrer, tasted it, frowned, and added more sugar.

Carol, who was setting out paper plates and cups, said to Molly, "Isn't it just terrible? I've known Jasper and Eileen for thirty years." She was in her sixties and wore her hair probably the same way she had in the Sixties, long and parted on one side.

Molly nodded. "Jasper was so supportive to me back when I was getting started," she said. "I remember when I didn't even make my booth rental my second year at the Georgia fair. Jasper encouraged me to keep at it. 'You won't get rich,' he said, 'but you'll have a heck of a great life.'" She felt a sudden wave of emotion. "I think he did too," she said in a low voice.

"That's right." Carol patted Molly's arm.

"The coffee's really good, Carol."

"I always get it from a local café on Central. They make the best coffee in the world. No cheap coffee for ABOG." Carol smiled with pride.

"I'm glad our dues are going for a good cause," replied Molly.

Jay popped up beside her, chewing. "So, what

happened? You just pulled into the parking lot and saw him laying there?"

Molly sighed. "Not exactly." She recounted the events of last night as briefly as she could.

Jay said, "Wow." He turned to Emma. "Are you two some kind of magnet for dead bodies?"

Emma snapped, "I certainly hope not!" She turned to Molly. "I'm going to get my tea and go over there." She gestured to the table farthest from where they stood.

Elliot came up to the coffee urn and proceeded to refill his paper cup. "Terrible about Jasper, wasn't it?"

Amy, a young book dealer who had a shop in Conyers with her husband, came up and said, "How awful for you. You actually found Jasper—dead."

Molly said. "Yes, Emma and I found him." She looked across the long tables to see Emma sitting at the end of one, digging into the pancakes, a mug at her side.

"I'm going over there to eat," Molly said and hastily made her way over. She sat across from her friend. "These pancakes are really good," she remarked.

"They are." Emma took a swallow from her mug. "And Carol brought Irish Breakfast tea. She thinks of everything."

Molly looked around. "All the ABOG members who came to Florida are here. Carol was asking questions, and Amy was trying to grill me, and Jay was being obnoxious as usual. Harry's over there, and Elliot is talking to Lynda."

"I don't think I've met her. She doesn't come to meetings much, does she?"

"Her bookstore is out in Peachtree City," Molly said.

Emma peered at the blonde woman as she swallowed the last of her tea.

Harry, the president, called the meeting to order. The business of ABOG was quickly taken care of, and the book dealers once more began to talk.

Not wanting to talk any more about finding Jasper, Molly went to her booth. She was glad to get a moment alone. She began to straighten her shelves, and then it was time to greet her first customers. She noticed Detectives Rodriguez and Greenfield in two different booths. She hoped they wouldn't come to talk to her since she had an appointment with them on Monday.

About two hours later, Emma walked up. "How's your show going?"

"So-so," Molly said. "I've been answering questions most of the morning. How about you?"

"Me too. I'm kind of overwhelmed by it all. At least Ari's should bring lunch soon." Ari's was a local Greek sandwich and salad place that offered catering services to the book fair. "What are you having?"

"Greek salad."

"I'm getting a falafel sandwich this time."

"How's *your* show?" Molly asked

"I sold a couple of early twentieth century illustrated classics about an hour ago. A young woman whose grand-mother had similar copies." Emma sat in Molly's other folding chair. "But nothing since. Old Grumpity Grump drifted by, scowled at me, fingered my Poe *Tales*, and ga-lumphed off."

Old Grumpity Grump's real name was Jefferson Davis Wilkes. His booth, appropriately named Old Virginia Books, contained Civil War and 19th century. He was a long-time bookseller from Richmond and had a reputation for irascibility, particularly towards female booksellers. Molly had been in his booth earlier when a grim-faced, graying man made a beeline toward the Thomas Dixon trilogy, what she liked to call "books for unreconstructed Confederates."

Emma said, "Grump has a 1935 edition of Poe, illus-trated by Rackham, prominently displayed and guarded by a large bronze raven. Same edition as mine, but his is signed by Rackham."

"You're lucky he didn't fuss at you for some breach of protocol."

"I try to smile and say nothing to annoy him. However, I did see a nice copy of *With Lee in Virginia* in his booth. Thinking about buying it."

"Nevermore!" Molly croaked.

Emma crossed her legs and swung her foot, sandal dangling.

Molly looked up the *St. Petersburg Times* online. "Here's the story. St. Pete police announced they found Jasper's body by a dumpster close to downtown last night." She scrolled down on her phone. "This also says he may have had dementia."

"Nothing new."

Molly handed the phone to Emma, who read the article for herself.

" '*Et in Arcadia ego,* '" murmured Emma.

Molly gave her a half-smile. "Meaning?"

"Even in Arcadia."

"Is the book fair Arcadia?"

"For some, it is." Emma sighed. "I hate to see it revealed as just like the rest of the world." She shook her head and stood up.

They both jumped as Kitty's voice burst out over the loudspeaker. "Dealers, those of you who ordered from Ari's, he's in the back with your lunch."

"Want me to pick up your sandwich?" Molly asked. "What else did you order?"

"A root beer. Thanks, that would be great." And Emma rushed back to her booth.

Chapter 7
The Missing

Johanna Spyri, Heidi, *Boston: Cupples, Upham, & Company, 1885. First American edition. Originally published in German in 1880 and 1881. Gold cloth stamped in black, tan flower-patterned endpapers. Title pages printed in red and black.*

When Emma returned to her booth, two Bobbsey Twins books were in her chair with a business card from Jerry of Over the Hills and Far Away. Before writing them up, she ran her eyes over all her shelves. She sat down and wrote up a receipt for The *Bobbsey Twins at Spruce Lake* and *The Bobbsey Twins at Windmill Cottage*, giving him the standard dealer's discount of twenty percent. Not a major sale—the two books were only twenty dollars each—but even small sales added up.

Mignon was browsing Emma's booth with a short dark-haired young man. He gave Emma a wide grin and held out his hand. "Hi, I'm Nick. With Ari's."

She shook his hand. "Nice to meet you, I'm Emma."

"You got some cool books."

"Thank you. I enjoy your food. So glad you all provide

it for dealers."

"My pleasure. Well, I better get back to help my brother with the food. Just wanted to visit with Mignon here." He walked, not too quickly, towards the back of the Coliseum. Mignon wandered off.

Emma was straightening her shelves when a heavyset man, about sixty, wearing a tropical shirt with large red hibiscus blooms stepped into her booth, two books under his arm. He squinted at the sign that read, "Clarke's Collectibles."

"Emma?" he asked. "Antonio."

"Hi, Antonio." She looked at the books he was carrying and saw the word *Alice*. "Is that my book?"

He held them out. "Jasper Ross left two books in my booth that might be yours."

Emma felt a surge of excitement. "These are my books!" She seized *Alice in Wonderland* and *A Child's Garden of Verses*.

"Jasper stopped by my booth Friday afternoon. He was pleased to have gotten some nice books from you. He couldn't remember your name, said Anna or Emmy or something. When I couldn't find anyone with either of those names, I just looked for children's book dealers and thought 'Emma' was close enough." He ran his hand through his thick, wavy, gray hair.

"Did he have more books with him?"

"I don't remember."

Emma hugged her found books. "Thanks, Antonio."

He nodded. "Glad to help." He raised his hand in a half-hearted salute and shambled off.

"Hey, Emma." Molly appeared carrying a paper bag. "Root beer and falafel sandwich."

"Thanks, Mol. Hey, you'll never guess what happened! A friend of Jasper's just brought back two of my missing books: *A Child's Garden of Verses* and *Alice*. Jasper had left them in his booth."

"That's great! I'll bet the other three will show up soon."

Emma crossed her fingers. "What do I owe you?"

Molly waved her hand. "You can do something for me some day." She was a little dressed up for the second day of the fair, wearing some newish dark denim jeans and a lavender V-neck sweater. A tiny pink silk blossom peeked out of the V. Emma envisioned a pink camisole underneath and felt her face flush.

"Gotta run," Molly said. "I'm going to eat my salad at the booth even if we are supposed to go to the eating area." She strode away.

Emma thought she probably should ask Eileen if she wanted to buy the books Antonio had brought, but not today.

As soon as she had arrived at the Coliseum that morning, she had asked Kitty if anyone had turned in any books. She decided to go back and ask Kitty again.

"Hi, Kitty, two of my missing books have been returned. Could you ask over the intercom if anyone has these?" Emma handed over a list.

"Okay. But most dealers know to bring any merchandise left in their booth to the front desk."

Emma said, "But Antonio brought two of my books directly to me."

Kitty said, "I'll make an announcement that anyone who sees books that don't belong to them should bring them to the front desk. Can I keep this list?"

"Sure."

Kitty nodded briskly. "Anything else?"

"I was just wondering—could you tell me what the security is here?"

"During the day, people have to show their receipts as they go out. We have two plain clothes security people who walk through the building during the fair. At night, we lock the building and have two off-duty officers outside and one inside. As you know, this building is tight."

Emma thought of the chaos yesterday as dealers and porters pushed rumbling carts loaded with boxes of books up the concrete ramp in back and through the wide double doors into the hall. The front doors had also been wide open, letting in heat from outside and people tramping in and out. Anyone could have come in. But she didn't want to contradict Kitty, so she said, "Thank you, Kitty. You're doing a great job."

Emma returned to her booth to see Jerry from Over the Hills and Far Away standing by her table. "Hey, Emma," he said, a worried frown on his normally calm, good-humored, pink face. "You haven't seen my *Hobbit*, have you?"

"What? That first edition?"

"Yeah. I can't find it anywhere." Jerry's voice sounded close to panic.

"No, I haven't seen it, not since I was in your booth."

"I just bought it," said Jerry. "A real find. It was right there on the stand, and when I came back from picking up my lunch, it was gone."

A loud voice boomed, "You don't just take a book out of a booth!"

Emma and Jerry both jerked around to see Old Grumpity Grump charging toward them. "If you want to be a bookseller, you need to observe the proprieties." He shook his finger at Emma, who took a step back.

"I don't know what you mean, Mr.—" Emma couldn't remember his real name. "I certainly haven't taken any books from your booth."

"If you didn't, who did? I saw you looking at my Poe."

Emma and Jerry just stared at him. Under their silent scrutiny, the bearded man's scowl turned uncertain.

"What book was taken, sir?" Jerry asked politely.

Grumpity exclaimed, "Poe's *Tales of Mystery and Imagination!* Illustrated by Rackham. I'm going to report this to the manager at once." He charged away toward the front desk.

Jerry stared at Emma. "Are people taking books from booths, right in plain sight?"

Emma shook her head in disbelief.

"Oh, my gosh, I'd better get back." Jerry hurried away.

Left alone again, Emma went through her shelves methodically. Nothing seemed to be missing. At the thought of the books Jasper had taken, she slumped farther down in her chair, her spirits sagging. *Is this going to turn out to be a bust of a book fair? I was on top of the wheel of fortune when I thought I had made that sale to Jasper. Now it's midday Saturday, and all I have so far are small sales and big losses.*

Chapter 8
Return to Your Booth

Comtesse de Ségur, Old French Fairy Tales, *Philadelphia: Penn Publishing Company, 1920. Illustrated by Virginia Frances Sterrett. First edition. Black cloth boards with pastedown color plate, gilt lettering. Manila colored end-papers with orange design of castle and birds in flight. Fourteen color plates with red captioned tissue guards. Black and white illustrations throughout.*

As usual, Molly couldn't finish her Greek salad, so she wrapped it up and slid it under her table just in time for a young couple to place a large stack of her occult books on her table.

"Hi," she greeted them. "Good to see you again." They had purchased a first edition of Madame Blavatsky's *Secret Doctrine* last year.

The pink-haired young woman beamed. "We always come to your booth first. We plan on how much we have to spend and end up spending most of it here. Then we look at the rest of the fair."

Molly was completing the sale when she heard Kitty's anxious voice over the loudspeaker: "Dealers, return to your booths!"

Dealers were scurrying in every direction. In the twenty-plus years that Molly had been going to book fairs, she had never heard such an announcement. Dealers spent large chunks of time in other booksellers' booths, shopping, visiting, browsing, making supper plans, and generally enjoying long distance friendships and professional relationships.

Each book fair was its own little village where the denizens came from other parts of the country and, sometimes, other parts of the world. At most book fairs, once a dealer had a booth, they had the same location every year unless they wanted to upgrade to a bigger booth or a corner one if it came open. If they had to skip a year, they lost their place. Molly made sure she didn't have to miss a year in St. Pete because she liked her corner space where repeat customers knew where to find her.

Reenie Allen, eyes sparkling with excitement, leaned over from her chair in the aisle. Reenie, half of the couple from St. Augustine whose booth stood directly across from Molly's, was a constant source of news. Wisps of gray hair were escaping from her bun, and her feet seemed to be sliding out of her Birkenstocks. "I heard about those books that were stolen!"

"What books?" Molly asked.

"Four dealers had books stolen. Jeff, Jerry, Lynda, and Bob. Today! I'll bet it's that guy who's always here, you know, the one in the blue sport coat?"

Over the years, Reenie had sidled up to Molly and let her know that the guy in the blue sport coat had been spotted. She was sure he was stealing books. Molly wondered why a book thief would wear the same coat every year. But maybe it had hidden pockets like the jacket worn by a book thief who was killed last year in Atlanta.

Molly thought she had better call Emma to see if any of her books were missing. She was interrupted by a woman wearing a green paisley shawl who rolled her wheelchair into the booth. She came by every year and liked coffee-table gardening books, so Molly made sure the few she had were on the table within easy reach.

"I have a new book on fuchsias and one on orchids," Molly said.

"Where?" the woman asked eagerly.

Molly showed her, and while her customer perused the orchid book, a little Chihuahua peeked out of the shawl. "Hi, Mickey," Molly cooed. Without saying a word, the woman put down the book and wheeled away. *Oh, well,* Molly thought. *After all that enthusiasm. Maybe she got miffed because I called her dog by name and not her.*

Molly had a quick phone conversation with Emma, who assured her that no more of her books were missing. Molly turned to Reenie and asked, "Do you know what books they were?"

"Jeff was yelling about a Poe."

A short, straight-backed man in a vest came into Molly's booth. She recognized him as Fritz, the husband of a dealer who sold miniature books. He also performed undercover security. "Buyers are missing books. So many that we're convinced thieves have taken them," he announced, speaking with a slight German accent. "The ones that were stolen were displayed like this while the dealers were out of their booths." He indicated one of Molly's bookstands. "That's why we must stay in our own booths."

Usually, dealers watched out for the booth of a neighbor who was away, as Reenie sometimes offered to do. But a savvy stealer could probably slip away unnoticed.

"For how long?" Molly asked. She hadn't had much time to look around, but now that she'd made a couple of big sales, she felt eager to find something new.

"For today, maybe until closing time."

"Okay, thanks, Fritz."

He went across the aisle to talk to Reenie and her husband, Paul, an affable but quiet man. Reenie asked Fritz lots of questions about what books were taken and from which booths, and if they had followed the man in the blue sport coat. Molly thought, *at least they have two people in their booth, so one can stay there while the other wanders around.* She looked at her shelves and didn't see anything missing. Loud voices assailed her ears from the booth behind hers.

"Is this to protect us from theft or to keep us as suspects out of other booths?"

Molly didn't recognize the voice, but heard Fritz say, in the same tone he had used with her, but a little louder, "Sir, we want you in your booth to protect your books. The police have been called."

"Police?" A woman's voice sounded alarmed.

Molly walked around to the outside of her booth, pretending to check on the shelves facing out. She saw Fritz's back, and facing him, the married couple who dealt in foreign language books in English translation and in books made into movies. Her name was Margot.

"Yes, ma'am," Fritz answered. "Several dealers have had their books stolen, and we want the police to come and take their statements."

"May I have a list of stolen books?" Margot asked. "I'll notify the ABAA so they can put out a notice to all booksellers in case someone tries to sell them." The Antiquarian Booksellers Association of America was diligent in notifying its members about stolen books.

"We are still compiling a list," Fritz said. "Please check to make sure if any of your books are missing, and let Kitty know."

After Fritz moved down the aisle, Molly heard the woman exclaim, "It can't be one of us!"

"Dealers!" Kitty's voice rang over the sound system.

"Please exit only through the front door. The rear doors have been locked. Repeat. Exit only through the front door. All rear doors have been locked."

"We're on lock-down!" said a familiar woman's voice.

Molly turned around to see Patricia. She and her husband had a booth at the end of the aisle.

"Hi, Patricia," Molly said.

"Hey! How are you doing?" Patricia gave Molly a hug. She wore a scarf in greens, yellows, and reds wrapped around her dreadlocks. The bold colors set off her dark brown skin and the pepper-and-salt curls that peeked out, framing her face. She wore a Daughters of the American Revolution pin on her lapel.

"I'm doing all right," said Molly. "What about you and Darrell? How's business?" Patricia and her husband ran a bookstore in Tampa.

"The shop's fine. We left our daughter to run it. Darrell's in the booth now. We're not going to take our eyes off our books until this thing is settled." Patricia shook her head. "Wasn't that sad about Jasper? He had dementia, or so I heard."

"I believe so," said Molly. She hoped Patricia wouldn't ask her anything about finding Jasper's body. She was tired of answering questions, so she quickly asked, "Have you done any more genealogy research?" Patricia was an avid genealogist who had written a book about her African and European ancestors.

"Yes!" Patricia exclaimed. "And I just went to a DAR meeting last weekend." She pointed to her lapel pin. "You know, I integrated the DAR chapter here, and I'm trying to recruit more black women to join. After all, so many of us are qualified to belong."

"That's certainly true."

"The problem, of course, is documentation. We have plenty of family stories, but they're not always written down. Black people didn't always have birth certificates, but I was able to track my European ancestors."

As they talked, Molly glanced up and down the aisle. The man in the blue sport jacket hurried by at the end of the row. A clutch of teenagers poured in and made straight for the Theosophy shelf. "Hey," said one, lifting down a volume. "Look at this. Vegetarianism." They crowded around as he leafed slowly through the volume.

Chapter 9
At the End of the Day

George MacDonald, At the Back of the North Wind, *Philadelphia: David McKay, 1919. Illustrated by Jessie Willcox Smith. Tan cloth with black lettering. Pastedown illustration on front cover. Illustrated endpapers. Eight color plates.*

At four o'clock Emma sat, arms crossed, watching the stream of shoppers as the crowd thinned out. She straightened her business cards, fanned them, and looked over her receipt book at her sales. She had not sold nearly as many books as she had hoped. She got up to replace *The Water Babies*, illustrated by Jessie Willcox Smith, on a wooden stand with another of her favorites, the first American edition of *The Wind in the Willows*.

Jay breezed past. He stopped, reversed, and spun into Emma's booth, his red hair tousled. "So, how's it going?" He shared with Harry one of the alcoves that lined the hall, more expensive than booths on the floor because they were more visible.

"Okay," Emma said. She thought, *he's just like Tigger in* Winnie the Pooh, *always bouncing around, while Harry is like slow-moving, honey-loving Pooh.*

"This lockdown sucks, doesn't it?" Jay said, rocking from his heels to his toes.

Emma nodded. "Sure does. But at least you and Harry can take turns shopping. I can't leave my booth."

He zeroed in on her small row of graphic novels. "Any *Black Panthers*?"

Emma shook her head. "I don't have any comics."

"You had some books stolen, didn't you?" Jay's ever-moving eyes raked her shelves.

"No. Five were taken by Jasper to show Eileen. But I got two of them back; they had been left in a booth. Three are still missing."

"I was lucky, I guess. None of mine have been taken. I heard it was mostly illustrated books. Are you sure no more of yours are gone?"

Emma snapped, "Of course I'm sure. The ones taken were on stands."

"I didn't mean anything by it." He smoothed down his hair, but it sprang back up. "Guess I'd better get back to the booth. Harry's holding down the fort. See ya."

What's the matter with me? Emma thought. *I'm on edge, and I don't want to talk to anyone. I just want this book fair to be over before anybody else dies. And I want my books back.*

⌘⌘

Molly fidgeted. She was not used to sitting in her booth all day.

"Molly?" Reenie leaned over. "If you want to look around, I'll be glad to sit in your booth while you're gone. Paul can watch our booth." She gave her husband Paul an inquiring look, and he nodded, settling down farther into his chair.

"Thanks!" Molly didn't waste a moment. She was out

of her chair and on her way. She wandered into Kraken's Lair. Chris Kraken sold comics, graphic novels, and prints. His tall, thin frame made a C-shape in his tilted-back chair. His shoulder-length hair had been pulled into a slick, black ponytail.

"Hi," she said. "You have some LGBTQ+, don't you?"

"I do. The books are on that shelf over there, and the ephemera is in that box." He put all four of his chair legs on the ground. "By the way, someone lifted my Robert Mapplethorpe book. Would you keep an eye out for it?"

Molly said she would and started to leaf through the box of prints and illustrations, all neatly sheathed in plastic. Flyers, posters, and brochures from the 1970's and earlier: leftist, Black Panther (the political movement, not the comics), and gay materials. She flipped through some gay male erotica prints and recognized the art of Tom of Finland, burly men with bulging muscles and crotches. Then she saw some other drawings, more elaborate. "These are beautiful," she murmured.

"Yeah, aren't they?" answered Chris, looking up from a comic book. "They're by a little-known Scandinavian artist named Gunnar Knut. Early twentieth century."

Molly paged through the drawings. They were like artistic comics, a little Japanese-inspired, clearly erotica of different flavors. Bodies partially nude, swirling draperies, wild patterns, dramatic use of space and line. Blue-faced demons, fairies, winged beings, pale girls, muscular men, sorcerers, witches. Exaggerated bodies, emotionally intense, stylized, just this side of elegant porn. They were disturbing and beautiful at once. She put them back, saying, "Thanks."

After a stop at the bathroom, Molly dropped by Emma's booth. "How's it going?"

Emma looked up and smiled. "Molly, I'm so glad to see you! How did you get out of your booth?"

"My neighbor offered to watch my booth so I could shop around."

Emma sighed. "Lucky you. I haven't had many sales, I can't leave my booth to shop because of this stupid lockdown, and I'm tired of reading my email. I've started looking up my own books to see if I need to change the prices." She held up her tablet so Molly could see the screen. "Here's *East of the Sun*. According to this, I ought to have marked it for two thousand more than I priced it for."

Molly peered at the picture on the screen. "That's the frontispiece, isn't it?"

"Yes," Emma said. "That color plate of the knight opposite the title page is my favorite of all the plates in the book."

"Beautiful," Molly said. "What an artist Nielsen was."

"Did you know he went to Los Angeles in the 1930's and was under contract to Disney for a few years? He worked on the 'Bald Mountain' section of *Fantasia*."

"I didn't know that."

"But he was let go because he worked more slowly than the fast-paced, assembly-line style of Hollywood."

"Typical, but so unfair."

"He lived his last years in poverty in L.A., painting murals on school buildings and churches for a pittance and accepting charity from his friends."

"What a shame."

Emma clicked to leave the web page, but Molly's hand reached to stop her.

"Wait! Go back a minute."

Emma returned to the page. "What is it?"

Molly leaned closer. "Would you make that picture bigger?"

Emma did, and they both leaned forward to look at a drawing of a prince bending to kiss a princess, his many-colored cape swirling around them both.

"That reminds me of something I just saw," Molly said. "Have you ever heard of an artist named Gunnar Knut?"

Emma shook her head. "No. Is he a book illustrator?"

"I don't think so. I just learned about him. Kraken has some prints of his." Molly gestured towards the screen. "But the prints look so much like these." Molly gestured toward the screen. "Just a little more—erotic, if you know what I mean."

Emma raised her eyebrows. "Nielsen isn't what I would call erotic."

"Knut's prints look like a cross between Nielsen and Tom of Finland. With a touch of Beardsley thrown in."

"Sounds interesting," Emma said. "I'd like to see them."

"Why don't I watch your booth while you go over and take a look?"

Emma jumped up. "Thanks! This will help keep me from going stir-crazy, if nothing else."

Molly pointed. "He's down at the end of my aisle."

Emma quickly walked off, tablet under her arm.

Molly watched her walk away, her dark blue leggings showing the contours of her legs. *The erotic takes many forms*, she thought.

☙❧

Emma returned to her booth after about ten minutes, excited about the prints she had just seen. "Molly, you're right! Just this side of porn—"

She stopped as she saw two women standing in front of Molly, who was putting four Little Golden Books into a bag.

Emma switched mode lightning fast. "Hello!" she said warmly. "Glad to see you again."

"We just love Little Golden Books," said one. "I'm so pleased you have some this year. I remember the teacher had all of these in the classroom when I was in first grade."

"Did you take a look at *The House at Pooh Corner*?"

"Yes," said the other woman. "Maybe we'll come back tomorrow. I have to ask my daughter if she'd like it for her little girl. She's four."

Emma hoped if the daughter did buy *Pooh Corner*, she wouldn't put it into her little girl's grubby hands until the child was much older. She said diplomatically, "She's just the right age to be read to."

After saying farewell to the women and the Little Golden Books, Emma sank down in the second chair. "Whew! I hope they didn't hear me say 'porn.'"

Molly grinned. "Pooh meets porn. So, what do you think about Gunnar Knut?"

"His work does look an awful lot like Nielsen's."

"Do you think it might be ol' Kay under another name?"

"Maybe so. But it's surprising that nobody has discovered it."

"Unless they have." Molly was already typing in "Gunnar Knut." Emma leaned close over her shoulder. "Nothing shows up," Molly murmured.

"That's odd," Emma said.

A family with two children entered the booth, a boy around seven, auburn-haired and silent, and a girl, about nine, dark-haired and willowy. "Oh, look!" said the girl. "*Anne of Green Gables*." She zipped over to the book on the wooden stand.

"You can take it down and look at it," Emma said. The girl looked old enough to know she should treat a vintage book with respect.

The boy glanced around and saw a row of small books. He went to them and stared. He had zeroed in on a set of *The Spiderwick Chronicles*, a modern fantasy series for middle graders by Holly Black with detailed line drawings by Tony DiTerlizzi.

The mother said, "Ask if you can look."

He turned to Emma with a mute question.

"Go ahead," she said.

The boy carefully pulled one of the books off the shelf and opened it.

In a few minutes, after conferring with their parents, the two children brought over their choices. The boy held the full set of *The Spiderwick Chronicles*. When Emma took them from him to bag up, she saw his fingers twitching as though they couldn't wait to hold the books again.

The girl carefully placed *Anne of Green Gables* by E.M. Montgomery and *Ballet Shoes* by Noel Streatfield on the table. Emma winked at the kids as she handed the father the laden bag.

As the family left, Emma said, "I just love to see that."

Molly said, "Me too."

The two shared a secret smile of bookseller satisfaction.

❦❦❦

At five o'clock, Molly pulled her chairs in front of her booth, pushed a tote bag with supplies under the table drape, and picked up her jacket and purse. She went towards Emma's booth. Maybe her friend would like to have dinner at the Seafood Shack downtown.

But when she got to Emma's booth, she saw Jay and Harry talking to Emma. Harry wore a silver Zuni bracelet and another silver band around his graying ponytail. He was tall, a gentle giant kind of guy. Jay looked up. "Hey, Molly! Want to come with us to the Seafood Shack?"

Molly felt irritated. She had wanted to go to dinner with Emma, just the two of them. *But,* she thought, *if I go with them, I can sit by Emma, and maybe I can also find out more from the other booksellers about what's going on.* So, she said, "Sure." Emma looked away from Harry and smiled at her, and Molly's irritation vanished.

Walking toward the Seafood Shack, an informal place on Central Avenue with Harry, Jay, Darrell, and Patricia, they ran into Bob and Sharon of The Captain's Quarters in Chicago. Bob always looked like he'd skipped a day shaving. He had a receding hairline and thin brown hair. His books were what Molly called geezer stuff: war, hunting, and fishing.

"Hey," Bob said. "Where you guys going?"

"Hey, man, Seafood Shack. Wanna come?" Harry asked.

Molly groaned to herself. She didn't like being around Bob, but Sharon was okay. She was an artist and always wore vintage clothing that looked well put together.

At the restaurant, Molly grabbed the chair next to Emma. A tattooed server plunked down menus and asked, "Can I start ya'll out with some drinks?" Most of them ordered alcoholic beverages, and Darrell stuck with water. Darrell had retired from the Navy and still carried himself as if ready to salute. His hair was cut short with a shaved part line down the side. Quiet, he always had an easy smile.

"Terrible about poor old Jasper, isn't it?" Jay said.

Mumbles of, "yeah, terrible," "so awful," "so sad," went around the table.

Patricia asked, "Is his family okay? I mean—I'd be glad to contribute something if needed."

"I think Eileen, his wife, is all right financially," Harry said. "She's got her daughter and son-in-law who live here in Florida."

"How about a scholarship in his name, maybe to the Rare Book School or to CABS?" Jay suggested. CABS referred to the Colorado Antiquarian Book Seminar that was formerly held every summer in Colorado Springs. For the last few years, the seminar had been held in Minnesota, but the name was still CABS.

"Good idea," Molly said. She was disappointed in herself that she hadn't thought of that first. Murmurs of approval went around.

"What do y'all think about the missing books?" asked Jay.

Bob said, "They need to have tighter security here. Maybe we ought to hire our own guards—and make sure they're armed."

Patricia said, "We've already had one death. Do we really want a shoot-out?"

Bob said, "I think I'll bring my automatic tomorrow. Just in case."

"Do you think that's a good idea, Honey?" Sharon asked, her penciled brows drawn up in a worried look.

Bob ignored her, but his mouth tightened.

"That's not cool, man," Harry said.

"Well—" Bob started to speak but was interrupted by the server who brought their drinks.

So," said Jay. "To a successful book fair—and to catching the thief!"

They all drank. Molly's dark beer was malty with coffee overtones.

Patricia leaned over to Molly. "What do you think about all this? I'm one of the lucky ones who didn't have anything taken."

"Me either," Molly said.

Patricia asked, "All the books taken were illustrated, weren't they?"

"Yes, that's right," said Jay, "They *were* illustrated, lit or children's or books with old maps."

Molly felt a chill go up her spine as she remembered that some of her occult books had astrological or other illustrations such as spirit photography. Were they still on her shelf?

Jay enumerated who among the booksellers had been

stolen from. "Jeff Wilkes, Chris Kraken, Lynda Duvall of Here Be Dragons, Over the Hills and Far Away—what's that guy's name?"

"Jerry," put in Harry.

"And me!" Bob almost shouted. "My book of Civil War maps!"

They all nodded sadly. Jay cleared his throat and started to speak, but their food arrived.

Molly dug into her New England clam chowder and accepted a bite of salmon from Emma's salad. The table was quiet for a moment except for sounds of munching. Harry ordered another beer, and Emma another glass of wine.

"I think I know who the thief must be," Jay said.

They all looked at him.

"Must be that guy with the antique prints. He sells illustrations that have been cut out of books and matted." Several booksellers shuddered, and Harry made a warding-off "X" sign.

"You mean Stewart?" Molly asked. "I don't think he would steal anything, but he may know who else deals in prints."

"Has *he* had anything stolen?" Patricia asked.

"Don't know," Jay said, wiping his mouth and pushing away his empty plate. "I'll ask him tomorrow."

As they left the restaurant, Molly noticed Mignon Chambray sitting with a brown-skinned Latin man with a shaved head and crisp linen shirt. Their heads were bent toward each other as if they weren't on Central Avenue amidst pedestrians.

Chapter 10
Sunday

Robert Louis Stevenson, Treasure Island, *New York: Charles Scribner's Sons, 1911. Illustrated by N. C. Wyeth. Black cloth with paste-down color illustration on front panel, 14 color plates.*

On Sunday morning, Emma arrived at the Coliseum a little before nine o'clock. She went to the back door in hopes that someone would be there already and let her in. But after pounding on the tall metallic double doors, she went around to the front. And stopped short.

Four cardboard banker's boxes were stacked on the porch.

Her first thought was maybe one of the local dealers was bringing in more stock.

She climbed the steps and bent down to examine the boxes. Someone had scrawled "Returned Books" on the top box. They were taped shut. She thought she ought not to touch them, so she went to the door and pounded. "Anyone here?"

She heard footsteps, and a sturdy young man opened the door. "Book fair opens at ten."

"I'm a dealer," said Emma, pulling her ID lanyard out

of her purse. "They told us we could come in at nine. Is Kitty here yet?"

"I'll go get her."

In a few moments, Kitty appeared. "Oh, hi, Emma."

Emma pointed. "Do you know what these are?"

Kitty frowned. "No. Ron, would you get a dolly and bring these inside?"

Ron put them on the dolly with ease and wheeled his burden inside the Coliseum.

Kitty got a box cutter and opened a box. She pulled up the flaps.

"Poe!" shouted Emma. "That's Old Gr—Jeff Wilkes's illustrated Poe." She thought, *Maybe my books are here!*

Kitty took out books and stacked them on the counter. "Do you think these are the stolen books?"

"They have to be. But why return them?" Emma finished taking books out of the first box while Kitty cut open another one. Books covered the desktop and a few chairs by the time they finished. *But my books aren't here.* She felt a chill. *Where the heck are they?*

"This is incredible," Kitty said. "All's well that ends well!"

જીભ

Laughter and chatter, sounds of relief and joy came from all around Emma. Mignon came into Emma's booth and started perusing her wares. Emma hoped that Mignon was having a successful show and would be in the mood to buy something from her.

Emma asked, "Did you have anything stolen?"

"Um, no. You?" Mignon turned back to the books without waiting for Emma's answer. She picked up *The Wind in the Willows* and turned it over and flipped through it. "I have one in much better condition than this. I guess I should raise my price."

What is she talking about? Only a few chips are on the dust jacket and the pages are tight.

"Sad about Jasper," Emma said. "Did you know him for a long time?"

"Yes, I did." Mignon's voice didn't invite conversation. She held up an early copy of *The Adventures of Huckleberry Finn* illustrated by E. W. Kimble. "I'll get this." She put the book down and rummaged in her purse.

Emma was busy running the credit card when a shriek burst out, "Oh my god!" Emma and Mignon turned around. A woman's voice cried out, "No! Oh, no!"

Emma's first thought was that another dead body had been discovered.

But more screams and shouts could be heard all around the Coliseum. "My Poe!" "Not the Rackham!" "Oh, god, my Hans Andersen!"

As dealers congregated in the snack area near Emma's booth, what happened became clear. All the returned books had their color plates surgically cut out. Mignon slipped out of Emma's booth so quietly that Emma didn't even notice she was gone.

Booksellers were gathered around the tables, holding paper cups of coffee or tea. The tables held pastries. A small knot of book dealers stood in the booth next to Emma's, close enough for her to hear them, but they could not see her.

"I'd rather not have gotten it back than to see it without the plates." She recognized Lynda's voice. Her Hans Christian Andersen had been mutilated.

"Why?" asked Kraken. Emma had unpacked his copy of Mapplethorpe's photos.

Jerry said in a low voice, "To threaten us, has to be."

Jeff grumbled, "…not do like Jasper."

"Those fuckers!" Bob blurted.

Emma quickly pulled down *Alice in Wonderland*. The illustrations were all there—black and white, eccentric, dark, edgy. She slowly let out her breath. She picked up *A Child's Garden of Verses*. She let out another long sigh as she saw that the illustrations were also still there.

The dealers drifted back to their booths, leaving the area empty.

A pair of well-worn loafers with long denimed legs attached strode into her booth. The brown shoes stopped in front of Emma's lowered head.

She looked up to see Molly standing before her.

"Are yours…?"

Emma pressed her lips together. "No. Mine are okay."

"Thank goodness. Mine too. And I do have a couple with color plates. My Aleister Crowley *Book of Thoth* is the most expensive." Molly suddenly stopped. "But it wasn't taken. It's still on my shelf." She looked puzzled.

Emma said, "I heard some dealers say something odd. It sounds like they know who cut the pictures out of the books. *And* they said something about Jasper."

"What did they say about him?"

"Something about a threat, to not be like Jasper."

"So, the murder and the book mutilating are related!"

Emma said, "Do you think it might be the guy Jay mentioned who sells antique prints?"

Molly said, "I've known Stewart a long time. He wouldn't steal books. And he certainly wouldn't mutilate a book in good condition. But let's go see him."

As Emma and Molly approached Stewart's booth, called "Antique and Collectible Prints," they saw a few dealers clustered around the young man with the neatly trimmed beard.

Stewart looked anxious, pinned in and surrounded by stern faces. "Listen, guys," he said, gesturing, palms out, "if anyone came to me with a bunch of pages from books,

I'd be suspicious. I certainly wouldn't buy them."

"But you do sell plates that have been cut out of books, don't you?" asked Jay.

"I admit I have cut pictures out of books, but only books that are falling apart already! Only when the prints are all that's worth anything. I would *never* cut up a good, much less valuable, book. Never!" He looked from one dealer to another, an imploring expression on his face.

Molly felt uneasy. She hated to see anyone ganged up on. She was just about to speak when another dealer said, "You could make some good money from these illustrations, couldn't you?"

"No!" Stewart exclaimed. "I mean, yes, maybe someone could, on some of the books. If the prints were matted nicely. But no reputable print dealer would ever do such a thing. Whoever has done this has no respect for the value of what he has stolen."

The dealer still glared.

Stewart said, "Listen, I can give you names of local print dealers, if you want to contact them and ask if they've seen your illustrations." He pulled at his beard nervously. "Why don't I contact the ones I know in the St. Pete-Tampa area myself?"

"Good idea. Tell them to be on the look-out." The dealer's shoulders relaxed.

The woman who had already sent the list of stolen books to the ABAA said, "I'll amend the list to specify prints rather than books."

The atmosphere became a little less tense.

"Look, there's Fritz." Jay broke out of the clump of dealers and took off after the plain-clothes security guard. The others followed.

Molly heaved a sigh. "You okay, Stewart?"

"Yeah," he said, smiling a nervous smile. "I'm just as shocked as everyone else. After all, if someone is stealing prints out of books, they might steal my prints! I haven't found any missing, though."

"Yeah," Molly said. "It's a puzzle." She glanced at Emma and said, "By the way, Emma, this is my friend Stewart. He's from Sarasota."

"Pleased to meet you." Stewart reached out his hand.

Emma smiled and took it. "I'm Emma from Atlanta."

Molly said, "Let's keep our eyes open, shall we?"

All three nodded vigorously.

As they walked away, Molly said, "I've known him a few years. He used to be Susan."

Emma was surprised. "He was at the Georgia Book Fair, wasn't he?"

"Yes. Susan and I were acquaintances, bonding over—well, I guess being queer, although we never said anything. Then one year I saw her with facial hair. She noticed the expression on my face and kindly explained to me that she—he—was transitioning, and that his name was now Stewart. I really like him. I'd hate for him to get accused of something he didn't do. Not all the dealers are comfortable with Stewart, but he isn't keeping his secret anymore—no matter what anyone thinks." Her eyes seemed to hold a question.

"I think he's very brave to live as who he is."

Molly smiled. "Yeah. He is brave."

Emma exhaled and looked at her watch. "Seven minutes until ten o'clock. I'm going back to my booth. I want a minute alone before the doors open."

"You'll have more than a minute," Molly said. "We open at ten, but eleven is church time. We won't see many people 'til afternoon."

Chapter 11

Interrogations

A.A. (Alan Alexander) Milne, When We Were Very Young, *New York: E.P. Dutton, 1924. Illustrated by E.H. Shepard. Limited edition of 100 signed by the author, of a total edition of 500. The first appearance of both Christopher Robin and an early incarnation of Winnie the Pooh (in "Teddy Bear"). Green cloth spine and white cloth pictorial boards.*

The fair had opened at ten, but as Molly predicted, there wasn't much foot traffic. At least they weren't still on lockdown. Around eleven, she noticed a uniformed police officer talking to Jerry in Over the Hills and Far Away around the corner from her. The officer was working her way in Molly's direction.

"Ms. O'Donnell?" Molly heard the clipped female voice and almost dropped the book in her hand. Turning, she saw the young, uniformed officer in her booth.

"Yes, Officer," she replied.

"We understand some books have been torn up, defaced, at the fair. Have you had anything like that happen to your books?" The officer was short, with long blond hair pulled back with an elastic band.

"No, I haven't," said Molly. "Some of my colleagues

have, though."

"Have you checked all your books?"

"Most of them, the ones that have illustrations."

The woman handed Molly a card. "I'm Officer Mendoza. Have you seen any suspicious activity since you've been here?"

Molly shook her head. "No."

"Were you in your booth all day Saturday?"

"Most of the day, except when I went to get my lunch. I walked around a little to shop."

"What times were you away?"

"I went to get lunch around noon, and I'm not really sure about the other times. A couple of times in the morning and in the afternoon. I was gone maybe twenty minutes each time."

"Did you see anyone who looked suspicious?"

Molly shook her head. "No."

Officer Mendoza said, "Okay, let us know if you remember anything." She went on to the next booth.

Shortly after one o'clock, an influx of buyers began to pour in. Some were dressed up as though they had come from church. Others looked as though they had come from the beach. The exceptions were the black-clad youths with tattoos. Molly blessed them silently as a trio crowded into her booth, poring intently over her Blavatskys and Crowleys. One of them touched the vellum Waite on Rosicrucianism. Molly thought, *why were some books damaged and others not?*

After the shoppers left, Molly headed towards the snack bar.

Mignon was in line ahead of Molly.

"How's it going?" Molly asked.

Mignon shrugged. "Have the police talked to you yet?"

"Yes. They asked me to let them know if I remembered anything from yesterday that was unusual."

"Well, of course," Mignon said sharply. "But at a book fair, what *is* unusual? Somebody rolling through on a skateboard?"

Molly smiled politely. She didn't know quite how to respond to Mignon, who was sometimes unexpectedly sarcastic. She bought an arepa and went quickly back to her booth.

No one was there when she got back. After she ate her lunch, she went to the ladies' room.

As she passed Emma's booth, she glanced over, but Emma was busy processing a sale, so Molly waved and didn't stop. She was sure that Emma would have already searched through all her books, since she had several with color plates and was so compulsive anyway.

One her way back, on impulse she stopped at Over the Hills and Far Away. As usual, Jerry was sitting in a folding chair, reading. Molly stepped into the booth and ran her fingers over the spine of one of his illustrated classics. She noticed that his shelves seemed more sparsely populated than she remembered.

He stopped reading and looked up with a questioning expression.

She asked, "You had some books defaced, didn't you?"

He looked at her with no expression for a moment. Then he sighed and said, "It's pretty well known that I did."

"Not all your illustrated classics, though?"

"No, not all." His voice sounded tight. "Only a few of my most valuable. Ones that were on stands facing outward."

His tone seemed to forbid her from asking any more questions, but she pushed on. "Do you have any idea at all who might have done it, or why?"

He looked at her with that same unreadable expression. "No, I don't."

"I'm sorry." Her words sounded inadequate. She also

felt that something didn't feel right.

After a moment, Jerry went back to reading, dismissing her.

Molly walked back to her booth, thinking, *that was odd.*

♥♥♥

Around two-thirty, Molly decided she wanted to get another look at Kraken's Gunnar Knut prints. On her way, she stopped at Emma's. "I'm going over to Chris Kraken's booth to look at those Knut prints again. Can you get away?"

Emma jumped out of her chair.

At Kraken's Lair, Molly and Emma paged through the prints and each pulled out a few.

"Who is this Gunnar Knut?" Molly asked Chris. "We looked online and couldn't find anything."

"I don't know. They're quite something, aren't they?"

Emma said, "That's unusual not to find anything about an artist."

Chris shrugged. "Yeah, I guess so. All I know is, they started turning up a few years ago, and I really like them." He stood and started looking through the prints.

"They look so much like Kay Nielsen," said Molly, "except more erotic than anything by him I've ever seen."

"You know he was impoverished at the end of his life," Emma said. "Maybe he did this just to make some money. At that time, they would be considered even more risqué than now."

"Well, if that could be proved, mine would be even more valuable." Chris grinned.

Molly thought, *I should buy some now.* She looked through the prints in her hands and selected three. One print showed two women lying on an ornate bed, fully clothed except that their bodices were open, revealing their breasts.

One woman had small, firm breasts, and the other's were large and voluptuous. The other two prints showed male couples.

"I'd like to buy these." She put them down in front of Chris.

He nodded with satisfaction. "Good choices."

They passed Bob and Sharon's booth. In defiance of the book fair rule, they were both already taking books down from their shelves, in preparation for the announcement that the book fair was closed. Bob didn't look their way, but Sharon gave a tentative wave. Molly stopped and said, "I'm so sorry about what happened to your books."

Bob glared at her. "What business is it of yours?"

"Bob!" Sharon whispered.

Molly said, "I suppose it isn't any of my business. But I'm sorry anyway."

"I'm sorry too," Emma said.

Bob hesitated. "I'm just all riled up today. Something like that happening here. And security touted as being so great. False advertising, if you ask me."

Molly nodded. "Well, good luck. Hope to see you again next year."

Bob grunted and turned back to taking books off shelves.

Sharon nodded at Molly and Emma with a tired smile.

Molly wondered whether she was tired from the book fair or from dealing with Bob.

At four o'clock, dealers started packing up books into boxes, porters rumbled through the Coliseum pushing dollies, and Molly had finished filling out her evaluation and reservation form for next year's book fair. She hadn't taken long to pack since she had her books displayed in wooden boxes with handles. All the porter had to do was swing them down and stack them on the dolly.

She folded up her stands and stashed them in an extra

wooden box. Thank goodness, all her books were accounted for. Her porter arrived and swung her boxes onto a large, flat dolly. Molly followed him out the back doors, now swung open. The dolly rumbled down the ramp, the porter filled her van, and Molly gave him a generous tip. She prepared to drive to The Flying Dutchman. She would stay there tonight, go to the police station tomorrow to be interviewed, and drive back to Atlanta.

On impulse, she decided to go back inside the Coliseum. As she navigated the aisle, she felt a bit of sadness at seeing the small, temporary village of booksellers dismantled. *A book Brigadoon,* she thought. *But will it ever recover from this disaster and be the way it was?*

Emma was packing her books into cardboard boxes. She looked up, breathing hard from exertion, as Molly walked up. "I must get some of those wooden boxes like you have," Emma said.

"I'll give you the name of the guy who makes them." Molly said. "Hey, I don't guess you'd be interested, but if you are…"

"Interested in what?" Emma put down the stack of books she was packing and wiped her forehead with a blue paisley bandana.

"Well, since we both have to stay tomorrow to talk to the police anyway, I was just thinking about staying over a little longer. Just a couple of days. And since you're staying too, I was wondering if you'd like to stay with me at The Dutchman." She felt her face flush. "My room has two beds. We could just look around St. Pete."

Emma looked perturbed. "I've already added another night to my reservation."

"Oh." Molly felt deflated. She should have thought of that.

"But—I'd like that. I'll check out tomorrow morning and come over in time to get to the police station."

Molly felt her heart skip a beat.

"Actually, it sounds like a wonderful idea," Emma said. "I'd like to think about something besides this awful book fair."

Molly said, "I was also thinking we might…"

"Might what?"

"That we might just wanna poke around a little, try to find out some things. I've got some questions I'd like to discuss with you."

Emma said, "Are you proposing we try to find out who did all this?"

"Ah, yeah. Are you in?"

"I'm in."

Chapter 12

Marjorie Kinnan Rawlings, The Yearling, *New York: Charles Scribner's Sons, 1939. Signed/limited edition, signed by Rawlings and N.C. Wyeth. Limited to 770 copies. Blue-green cloth. Gilt lettering on spine, top edge gilt. Pictorial endpapers. Fourteen color plates plus two black and white illustrations by N.C. Wyeth.*

On Monday morning, Emma and Molly went to the St. Pete police station at nine o'clock. The station was a new glass building with an enormous abstract sculpture that reminded Emma of a pineapple. They walked into the building where an aluminum eagle's wing hovered overhead. The officer behind the metal desk took their names and directed them to sit. Two other people sat on folding chairs, one a man who slumped, eyes closed. The other was a young woman whose eyes darted around and whose ballet-slippered foot jiggled.

Emma heard her name called and followed the woman officer, who led her to a small office facing Detective Paul Rodriguez, whom she had met the night of the murder. He was wearing a plaid shirt and chinos and had on horn-rimmed glasses.

"So, you're the one who found the body," Rodriguez

said. He sounded conversational, as though he were making a statement about her about finding a lost purse or book. "Can you tell me again what happened?"

"We parked in the lot behind the Flying Dutchman. As I was getting out of the car—"

"Your car?"

"Yes, sir. I drove because I wanted to leave from the Dutchman to drive back to my own motel."

Rodriguez made some notes. "When and where did you see the victim?"

Emma described to him how Molly had seen what looked like a tan windbreaker behind the dumpster, and how she and Molly had gone to look at it.

"What made you go and look?" the detective asked.

"I thought that maybe I'd seen that tan windbreaker before. At first, we just saw a sleeve, and that made me remember Jasper and his windbreaker."

"Why did you remember the windbreaker?"

"Jasper came to my booth early Friday morning. I lent him some books to show Eileen. I remember wondering at the time why he was wearing a jacket when it was quite warm without the air conditioner."

The detective made a few scratches on his pad.

"Are you aware that he had dementia?"

Emma nodded. "His wife was worried about him. I guess he was getting into the habit of wandering off. She never saw my books, and I don't know what happened after he left my booth. He left two in Antonio Alvarez's booth and Antonio brought them to me. But three are still missing. I told the police officers about them, but they didn't seem concerned."

"We're homicide. I heard that several books were stolen from the book fair and returned without the pictures."

"The books are valuable," Emma said. "My most expensive book—one of the ones that Jasper took—is worth as much as my car! What if there is a connection?"

Rodriguez narrowed his eyes. "Do you think there is?"

"It just seems odd that Jasper never returned to his booth, and Eileen was worried about him, and that some very valuable books are nowhere to be found, and poor Jasper is dead."

"Do you have any idea who would want Jasper dead?"

"No, but I overheard a conversation among whose books were taken. One of them said, 'They did it to threaten us,' and another said, 'not be like Jasper.'"

"Hmm." The detective scribbled on his notepad. "I'll check with the officers who talked with the booksellers whose books were stolen."

He asked more about Jasper being in her booth and if she knew of other booksellers who had seen him before his disappearance. When she mentioned Antonio again, as well as Jerry, he took notes.

When he finished writing, Rodriguez slapped the notepad on the desktop, rose, and said, "That's all for now, Ms. Clarke. Are you planning on staying in St. Petersburg for a few days?"

"Yes, Molly O'Donnell and I are planning on a little sightseeing and visiting other booksellers." *And snoop a little,* she said to herself.

"That's good. I have your phone number." He handed her a card. "Call me if you remember anything else, no matter how unimportant it seems."

"I will."

He smiled. "That'll be all for now." He started to turn away but looked back. "And stick around 'til Friday, all right?"

♥♥♥

"Damn," Molly said when they were eating breakfast

while reporting to each other about their police interviews. "My cop said the same thing: stay around 'til Friday. Do they think we're rich? I'll have to pay my pet sitter almost double."

They were in a small diner near the police station that served breakfast all day. Formica tables, booths, plastic-covered menus, black-and-white checked floor tiles. Molly thought it looked much as it must have fifty years ago, with a few updates to the menu like tofu scramble, avocado toast, and tempeh bacon. She took a bite of her bagel. She loved the "everything" bagel, and was having one now, slathered with cream cheese and topped with thin-sliced lox.

"Mmm," she said. "Wish this place were closer to the Dutchman."

Emma nodded, mouth full. She was devouring her scrambled eggs, bacon, and fried potatoes, topped with house-made catsup, as though she hadn't eaten in days. She swallowed a gulp of Irish Breakfast tea and fixed her eyes on Molly. "Why did you ask Bob and Sharon about their books being mutilated? Almost as though you were rubbing it in."

"I asked a few dealers about what happened to their books. I thought their reactions were interesting."

"How do you mean?"

"Well, Jerry and Bob both said yes, but they sounded defensive. Chris Kraken reluctantly said yes." Molly took a sip of coffee. "Remember you heard Jerry say on Sunday morning that someone did it 'to threaten us.' He said 'us,' I'm sure of it. As though there were a group of booksellers who were targeted."

"I told the detective about it. What could the connection be? Jerry sells children's books, but Mignon and I didn't have any of our books vandalized." She ticked off on her fingers: "Kraken had a photography book. Grumpity and

Bob both sell geezer books. One was a map, and the other was plates. And Lynda of Here Be Dragons does fantasy."

Molly said, "I'm stumped. I can't think of any connection. And they all come from different parts of the U.S." She groaned. "I miss Blavatsky and Dmitri. When I call tonight, I'll ask my sitter to put them on speaker phone."

"Aroooo!" Emma mock-howled.

Molly laughed. "You sound just like them."

She finished her coffee. "But since we're staying until Friday, we have time to investigate this crime ourselves. Let's head to Tarpon Springs and check out that antique print shop."

Chapter 13
Tarpon Springs

A.A. (Alan Alexander) Milne, Winnie-the-Pooh, *London: Methuen, 1926, Illustrated by Ernest H. Shepard. First trade edition. Green cloth, gilt illustration of Christopher Robin and Pooh on the front board, gilt lettering on spine, top edge gilt. Orange dust jacket with illustrations on reverse side. Full page and text illustrations, illustrated endpapers with map of "100 Aker Wood... Drawn by me and Mr. Shepard Helpd (sic.)."*

They drove along the coastal highway in Emma's book-laden Volvo station wagon. After much internal debate, Molly had left her loaded van parked in the Dutchman's narrow lot. All the St. Pete and Tampa print dealers had been told to be on the lookout for the cutout plates, but Molly, searching on her phone, had discovered a few other dealers in prints along the west coast. They planned to go north to Tarpon Springs and if they had no luck there, they would head south to the other cities.

As Emma drove, they both craned their necks to see the Gulf of Mexico between the old apartment buildings with pelicans, kingfishers, and jumping dolphins painted on crumbly turquoise or pink stucco.

"There's a public parking lot." Emma pointed. "Let's get out and walk to the beach."

"Great idea, Emma. Way to be spontaneous!"

Emma playfully slapped at Molly's leg as she swerved into the parking lot. Pizza shops, ice cream stands, seafood shacks, and bars lined the beach. On Monday morning, there weren't a lot of people on the beach, but still Molly felt odd in her jeans and T-shirt. Luckily, she was wearing sport sandals, while Emma had on nice leather slides with a silver concho on each one. Molly leaned down to roll up her jeans and looked at Emma, who had been prescient enough to wear cropped pants.

"Emma?" She asked in what she thought might be her sultriest voice.

"Mm?"

"You know what I really really like?"

Emma looked at her. "What?"

"I like long walks on the beach."

"Oh, you do? You know what I like?"

"Candlelight dinners?"

"Of course!" Emma laughed. "How did you know?"

"I read your profile."

"You ass! I've never posted a profile."

"You're kidding."

"I wouldn't want to spend an evening with someone I didn't know, with both of us expecting some sort of romantic thing to happen."

"A couple of years ago, I read a lot of F looking for F profiles," Molly said, "but the ones I contacted never panned out to more than safe coffee dates."

"Why not?"

Molly shrugged. "Maybe I really didn't want them to."

"Then why waste your time?"

"Curiosity?"

"What I don't like are the clichés," Emma said. "Why

can't people be more original?"

"I wonder," Molly said, "what lesbians who live on the coast say in their profiles? Do they like long walks on the beach, or maybe long hikes in the mountains?"

"Ha!" Emma said. She took off her sandals and led the way into the foamy edge of the waves. She sighed and closed her eyes, tilting her head back. "Something about the sound of crashing waves wipes my stress away."

Molly turned her own face up to the sun. The sand was warm, and the water was cool. She let herself relax and put out of her mind anything except the feel of the sun on her skin, the light breeze off the water, the quiet presence of the woman walking beside her. She thought she caught a whiff of a light scent from Emma, maybe floral soap or bath oil. *How utterly pleasant*, she thought, *to walk with someone without needing to talk. It's as though we've known each other forever.* They walked along as the other beach walkers thinned out, leaving them almost alone with the sun and the water. They stopped walking when they reached a rope that stretched out into the sea.

"Guess this is the end of the public beach," Emma said.

They reluctantly turned around and headed back.

Molly's jeans were starting to get wet, so she stepped onto the white, dry sand where the waves ended. When they reached where they had parked, she saw outside showers, conveniently placed for beachgoers, where they rinsed off their ankles and feet.

"That was relaxing," Molly said as she slipped into the Volvo.

"Yeah. Thanks for being spontaneous with me."

They shared a grin as Emma pulled out of the gravel parking lot.

Along the coast were expensive newer hotels and condos. When they entered the town of Tarpon Springs, they drove by small stucco houses, probably erected in the early twentieth century.

Molly looked at the map on her phone. "Okay, in about two miles, turn right onto Sea Grape Avenue. The one before it is Taverna."

They pulled in front of a white building with a bail bonds office at one end and an empty space on the opposite end with signs for furniture and appliances. They parked in front and entered the main building through a door with a wavy glass window. Inside were several small businesses: radical books, a nail studio, several antique booths, and a door with "Comics and Prints" in scrolling type. Rows and rows of bins filled the center of the small space. The walls were covered with framed prints. The two women walked around the perimeter looking for any recognizable illustrations.

"Mol," Emma said and pointed at the wall where three matted color prints hung, each portraying children in clothes of the early twentieth century. The first showed a child in short blue overalls high in a tree, looking over a wall into a formal garden and to mountains beyond. The second portrayed a child in bed, eyes closed, under a white bedspread that blue-jacketed toy soldiers were marching across in formation. The third showed two children kneeling by a pond looking at their reflections. Emma whispered, "They're by Jessie Willcox Smith from *A Child's Garden of Verses*."

"Is that yours?"

Emma nodded. "It's one of the ones Jasper took but Antonio returned."

They started flipping through bins, spying several prints that Emma recognized as book illustrations.

"I'm going to the ABAA's website to find the list of books that had pictures taken from them," Emma whispered, pulling out her phone. Margot, true to her word, had already posted the titles of the mutilated books on the website. Emma stared intently at her phone for several seconds.

"Hi," came a woman's voice from the back. "Can I help you with anything?"

Molly turned to see a petite, gray-haired woman in jeans and a T-shirt coming toward them.

"We're looking for book illustration prints," Molly said. "Are these all you have?"

"I have more in the back."

"Can we see them?" Molly asked. "We're dealers."

"Sure." The woman gestured toward the door. "I haven't got around to pricing them yet. Just bought them day before yesterday. My name's Beth, by the way."

"I'm Molly, and this is Emma."

In the back, stacks of books, magazines, and prints covered every available desk or tabletop and cascaded over the floor. Beth gestured them over to a metal table. "Here are some prints I just bought. Haven't had a chance to price them or even put them in plastic sleeves. You can go through them, just handle them carefully. I'll check back in a few."

After Beth left, Emma nudged Molly. "Look," she said, pointing at a print. "Here's another Jessie Willcox Smith print—and here's the book listed on the ABAA website. Could we have found them this quickly?"

"Maybe," Molly said.

Emma lifted the delicate pages one by one and peered closely at each. She gasped. "Molly, look!"

Molly bent over to see in the dim light.

"It's the Poe illustrations," Emma whispered, voice shaky with excitement. "Old Grumpity's Poe illustrations."

"We can't prove it," Molly whispered back.

"I'd bet my eyeteeth they're the same!"

"Finding what you need?" asked Beth's voice from behind them. They both jumped.

"Yes—I mean, not quite," Emma said. "Where did you get these?"

Molly frowned. Emma had broken a book dealers' rule: one dealer doesn't ask another where they bought their stock.

But Beth answered cheerfully, "Yesterday, or maybe the day before, a friend of mine, an antique dealer from Tampa, came by and said he was selling some old prints. Said he'd been collecting them for a long time and didn't want them anymore. Gave them to me for a good price."

"The reason we're asking," Molly said quickly, "Is that some books were mutilated at the St. Pete Book Fair. Valuable books had illustrations cut out of them. We're looking to see if the illustrations might have been sold."

"What?" Beth exclaimed. "That's horrible! But my friend wouldn't do something like that. He's a reputable antique dealer. Been in the business for thirty years. When was the book fair?"

"This past weekend. The books were stolen on Saturday," Molly said.

"He said he'd had them for a while."

Emma handed Beth her phone. "Would you mind taking a look at this list on the ABAA website? These are the books the illustrations were cut out from. Just in case someone tries to sell them to you."

Beth peered at Emma's phone. She scrolled down. Then she looked up and frowned. "I'll keep an eye out for those prints."

"And spread the word with any print dealers or antique dealers you know?" Molly handed Beth her business card.

"Sure, I'd be glad to. This is as abhorrent to me as it is to you."

Emma was still rummaging through the table. "Look," she said in a low voice to Molly, "*Gulliver's Travels.*"

"Let's go, Emma."

When they got to the sidewalk, Emma said, "Why did we have to leave so quickly? You don't know that those prints weren't from the book fair."

"I doubt they were," Molly said. "She said her friend was a reputable dealer and that he had had them for a long time. And we need her help. If we start accusing her or her friend of stealing or cutting up books, we won't get any more information from her. We have to think carefully about this."

"Okay," Emma said softly. "Hey, you wanna get something to eat? We can plan how we're going to approach the next print dealer we talk to."

Molly grinned. "Here we are in downtown Tarpon Springs. Must be someplace nearby where the local shop owners eat lunch."

They strolled past antique shops and real estate offices, until, looking across the street, they saw a Greek restaurant called Mount Olympus.

"Look!" Emma pointed.

Molly said, "Greek food again?"

"I'm craving moussaka!" Emma called over her shoulder as they crossed the brick street.

Seated in Mount Olympus under a larger-than-life-sized statue of Athena holding a shield, they perused the menus. The walls were lined with pictures of celebrities posed with a short woman with shoulder-length dark hair and a beaming man with a large dark mustache. The booths had cracked plastic seats, but the napkins were thick, white cloth. Emma looked at the wine list. "They've got ouzo," she announced. "Maybe we could come back some evening?"

Molly nodded. She had eaten Greek salad for two days in a row, so when the waiter arrived, she ordered spanakopita.

Emma ordered moussaka and a side salad.

When the waiter brought their orders, Molly smiled to see Emma tuck into her moussaka with enthusiasm. She really did like food and seemed not to worry about keeping the pounds off her small, wiry body. Molly tasted a hot puff pastry roll—the feta and spinach deliciously melded.

The busboy came to clear their table. His name tag said "Nick."

Emma asked, "Hey, didn't you deliver to the Coliseum?"

He straightened up and smiled. "Yeah. Emma, right?"

"Yes. Good memory. This is Molly."

"Nice to meet you. How was your book sale?"

Molly and Emma both answered, "Good."

"Great to see you again." He headed toward the kitchen.

Molly said, "I don't remember him. I think it was another guy that I picked up the orders from."

"Nick was walking around with Mignon on Saturday. That's how I met him." Emma shot a glance at Nick who was talking to another young guy in a white apron. "Mount Olympus and Ari's must be owned by the same people."

"Maybe. Ready to head back down the coast toward Sarasota?" Molly stood up and slung her tote bag over her shoulder.

Emma picked up a brochure and a business card as they left. "Yes! Both Ari's and Mount Olympus are sister restaurants!"

"How long does it take to get there from here?"

"About two hours."

"Well, actually," Emma said, "with the beach and driving and visiting that shop, I'm ready to be in one place and rest for a while."

Molly checked the time. "Yeah, it would be close to five by the time we get there. And by the time we get to St. Pete, it's going to be rush hour."

"Why don't we go back to the room and go to Sarasota

tomorrow? I could take a nap after that full meal."

Molly thought, *A nap might be nice. Preferably in the same bed as Emma.* She remembered the feel of Emma's soft cotton nightgown the night they had spent, chastely, in Emma's bed after her house was trashed last year.

As they approached the Volvo, Molly saw Stewart walking toward the building that housed the print shop. She nudged Emma and pointed. "There's Stewart. I wonder what he's up to?"

"Maybe he knows Beth or the antique seller whose prints Beth had."

As Stewart disappeared through the door, Molly thought, *Here I am being suspicious.*

⌇⌇⌇

Back in the hotel, while Emma snoozed, Molly set directions in her phone for the print shops she had found in Sarasota and Fort Myers. She started looking for antique malls, but it would take at least a week to check out every booth. They could hit a few, though. Reenie and Paul had booths in three or four antique malls around the Tampa area. Reenie might know of someone who sells prints.

Her eyes fell on Emma sleeping, her arm thrown over her head and the dark strand of hair fallen over her cheek. Molly wanted to brush it back. Instead, she went to the Dutchman's front porch to call Reenie.

Molly settled into a wicker rocker and enjoyed the early evening breeze. Growing up in South Florida, she had looked forward to the first days that were warm enough for her to go to the beach even if the ocean would be cold. Some years she'd get her first sunburn in February, but that was far to the south of St. Pete. Molly called Reenie, who agreed to scout out the places where she stocked books for any illustrations.

After Molly ended the call, she watched the shuffle-board players at the senior center across the street. A sign announced: "English Country Dancing. All Are Welcome." Molly and her former partner had been to a couple of English Country dances, but it was hard to learn the steps. The dancing would be fun to watch, though. She noted that it started at six o'clock. Her phone read five-twenty. Emma had asked to be woken up before five-thirty, so Molly hurried upstairs.

Chapter 14
Good News for Once

C. S. Lewis, The Lion, the Witch, and the Wardrobe, *London: Geoffrey Bles, 1950. Illustrated by Pauline Baynes. First edition. The first book in the Chronicles of Narnia. Green cloth, silver gilt lettering on spine. In gray pictorial dust jacket. Color frontispiece and black and white illustrations throughout.*

Emma heard her phone ringing as she came out of sleep. She took a second to recognize the voice—Kitty, the book fair manager.

"Emma, I have good news! Two of your books have been found: *The Little Prince* and that one with the long title about Mulberry Street."

"Oh my god!" Emma sat bolt upright, clutching the phone with both hands. "That *is* good news." She swung her feet to the floor. "Are they all right? Where were they?"

"They look fine," Kitty said in a reassuring voice. "A dealer found them under her table. She dropped them by the shop before leaving town."

"How late are you open tonight?"

"Six-thirty."

Emma squinted at her phone. Nearly five-thirty. "Where

are you located?"

"We're on Second Avenue North. Sandpiper Books, in the green bungalow."

"I'll be right there."

Emma called Molly. "Guess what? *Mulberry* and the *Prince* have been found. Some dealer found them under their table. Where are you?"

"In the hallway. I just ran up the stairs."

Then Molly was in the room, and they hugged spontaneously.

Emma pulled away first, feeling suddenly flushed. "I can't believe it!"

"So where are they?"

"Kitty and Rick's store. Wanna go with?"

"Of course. I've never been there, I'm always so busy with the book fair."

They ran down the stairs and took the back way into the parking lot.

ლოლ

Emma pulled her Volvo up to the curb in front of the green Queen Anne cottage with lavender trim around the windows and door, a wrap-around porch, and a sign: "Sandpiper Books." A small sable palm grew on one side of the sandy yard, and a scraggly rosemary was on the other. A flagstone path led from the sidewalk to the porch, and a driveway curved around the house to a parking lot in back. Emma slid out and raced to the front door, Molly behind her.

Kitty stood behind the counter, wearing a sundress with a large flower print. "Emma! Your books are right here." She gestured to the counter towards *And to Think That I Saw It on Mulberry Street* and *The Little Prince*.

Emma grabbed them up and held them to her chest.

Then she set them down again, picked up the one on top, and leafed slowly through it. She let out a sigh. "They're okay. Nothing has been cut out."

Kitty gave her a pleased smile. "I'm so glad you got them back."

Molly said, "Hey, I'm going to go look around." She disappeared down an aisle.

"Now I can ask Eileen if she wants them," Emma said. "After all, Jasper did pick them out. By the way, who was the dealer who found them?"

"She's new," Kitty said. "Maria Morales. She set up for the first time this year."

Emma frowned. "Why did she wait til today? She must have found them on Sunday as we were all packing up."

Kitty shook her head. "Maybe they were under some other books or in a bag. She said her friend was helping her pack up."

"Well, thanks ever so much for helping me get them back."

"No problem!" Kitty turned, skirt swirling, and began to put books on shelves out of the boxes that stood about on the floor of the shop. "Sorry for the mess," she called out. "We haven't finished unpacking from the fair."

"I understand," Emma said. "I don't see how you can run a book fair and tend to a shop at the same time."

"Ricky works in the booth, and Dad helps out in the shop. You know, Dad's retired, if it's possible to retire from bookselling."

"Right," Emma said. She started to enter the aisle Molly had gone down but saw Molly hugging someone Emma didn't recognize. She sized her up: statuesque, long dark hair, attractive if a bit flashy with her purple tunic, black capri leggings, and dangly earrings. But maybe Molly liked flashy.

She heard Molly say, "Just a friend." *Obviously*

referring to me, thought Emma. *Yes, we are friends, but why do people say, "just a friend"? Friends are important, sometimes more important than lovers.*

Emma didn't want to look as though she were spying, but the illustrated classics were on the other side of the bookcase from where Molly and Purple Tunic were standing. And she actually did want to listen. Several times, she heard Molly say, "Well, I'm going to look around now." But the statuesque woman would ask a question or say something about her health problems. When Molly said something sympathetic and final-sounding as though she were trying to disengage, Purple Tunic returned with, "How's your mother?" Emma felt more annoyed than she liked to admit.

She decided to intervene. Molly was recounting how her mother's house had fared in the latest hurricane as Emma slowly approached, holding out a book.

"Molly…oops, sorry to interrupt, but here's some Kay Nielsen illustrations."

Molly turned around with a huge grin. "Oh, let's see." She glanced back at Purple Tunic. "Good to run into you, Carmen."

Carmen looked as though she would like to say something more, but instead she strolled toward the front of the shop, tunic swinging.

Why didn't Molly introduce us? Emma wondered.

"Gals," Kitty called. "We're gonna close shortly."

"Thanks again for the books," Emma called as they headed to the door.

Once in the car, Emma asked, "Who was that you were talking to?"

Molly groaned. "A mistake."

"Why was Carmen a mistake?"

Molly didn't answer right away. "I don't want to talk about it right now, if you don't mind."

Emma felt annoyed. "So why say it to begin with?" She drove onto the road.

"Forget I said anything." Molly folded her arms across her chest, her voice sounding flat.

"You ask me questions, and I answer them, most of the time." Emma tried to keep her voice matter of fact, but inside she was simmering. *Why was Molly suddenly putting up a wall?*

"That's your choice." Molly pulled out her phone and began to read.

Emma was so annoyed that she almost missed her turn back to the hotel. She swerved into the right lane just in time.

Molly exclaimed, "Watch out!"

Emma said through gritted teeth, "Don't tell me how to drive."

An uncomfortable silence grew between them. Molly still was absorbed in her phone.

Emma's anger subsided. She wished that they could just erase the last ten minutes. *What happened anyway?* "Hey, Molly," she began in a soft voice.

"What?"

"Look, I didn't mean for us to get into an argument. You're right, I shouldn't pry into your private life. I was curious about Carmen, I admit it. Saying something like 'a mistake' sounds kind of provocative. But I won't ask about her anymore," she said, gesturing as though to push Carmen away. "Just don't shut me out, okay?"

Molly turned off her phone. "I didn't mean to shut you out. I just can't discuss her right now." She sighed.

"We don't have to. Forget I asked."

Emma parked behind the hotel. Before she got out, she took a deep breath and turned toward Molly. "I'm sorry," she said. "The truth is—I'm—I just feel out of sorts. You know, I've lost money big time at this book fair. I bought

East of the Sun last year, and it was so much more than I had ever paid for a book before. I had to cash in CDs to cover all those books. I can't go on buying such expensive books."

Molly looked at her, listening.

"And you encouraged me!" Emma said. "Before last year, I thought I was paying a lot if I put two hundred dollars on a book. I never would have done it before."

"I thought *East of the Sun* was a good purchase. If you'd told me you couldn't afford it, I would have bought it myself since I do sell illustrated books. I asked if you wanted to buy it together and you said 'no.'"

Emma nodded. "You're absolutely right. It was entirely my choice to buy it. When you offered to pay half, I got greedy and wanted all the profit for myself." She paused. "I guess I don't know whether to blame myself or just accept the losses."

"Okay," Molly said, laying her hand on Emma's arm. "You bought the book, even though it was more expensive than any book you've bought before. But you bought it in the hopes of selling it for even more and making money. I thought I was helping you."

"I know," Emma said, looking straight ahead at the dumpster. The sky grew darker, and the dumpster looked sunk into shadow. Emma shivered.

"And you thought you had sold it at this book fair," Molly went on. "When you find it, you *will* sell it. And your investment will pay off."

"I'm just so worried that it's gone forever."

Molly smiled sympathetically. "The other books showed up, didn't they? This one will too."

Emma sighed. "And—this is worse—to tell you the truth, I'm envious of you. I envy you for having enough money to buy plenty of humongously expensive books when I don't. People say you aren't supposed to talk about money, but I'm going to. I don't have a lot, and I'm envious of people who can drop fifteen thousand dollars on a gorgeous book and not bat an eye. And that's the truth." She felt half ashamed and half defiant.

"I didn't have much money when I started," Molly said. "I was selling ten-dollar books at the Antique Market. It took a year or two before I dared to spend as much as one hundred dollars on a book. I will never forget the first time I spent that much. It was a first edition, first printing of *Other Voices, Other Rooms* by Truman Capote, 1948. I felt it was the right thing to do. I sold it at the next book fair for three times what I paid."

Molly's confidence seemed to infuse Emma with more of her own. "Thank you."

"Four of your books have already shown up. Just a matter of time until *East of the Sun* is back in your hands."

Emma was glad she had shared how she felt. And she was still curious about the mistake called Carmen.

Chapter 15
Stewart Again

E. R. Gaggin, An Ear for Uncle Emil, *New York: The Viking Press, 1939. Red cloth with blue drawing of a goose holding a doll. Blue lettering on spine, decorative endpapers. Dust jacket with color illustration of two children in Swiss mountain clothing. Eighty-three black and white illustrations by Kate Seredy. Story of a boy doll who gets turned into a girl doll.*

Molly sniffed the armpits of the T-shirt she had put on the day before. It had been intended for the drive home. She had no idea she'd be staying so long after the book fair ended. Emma was wearing a blue floral print sundress and her leather concho slides and looked elegant as usual.

Molly said, "Think we could find a laundromat later? I'm running out of clean clothes."

"Sure." Emma brushed her hair forward, using her fingers to fluff it out.

Maybe it would be better to wear the T-shirt I wore on the drive down, Molly thought. She dug through her suitcase and pulled out a light pink shirt with "Too Many Books Are Just Right" emblazoned across the front over a teetering stack of books.

"I picked out a print shop and two antique malls that have print dealers in Sarasota." Molly held up her phone. "Shall I give you the phone and you can navigate?"

"Actually, I would prefer a map. Old-fashioned of me, I know."

"I know, you're a Luddite," said Molly.

❦

When they arrived in Sarasota, they went first to West Coast Prints and More. As soon as they stepped inside, they saw Stewart, dressed in baggy, knee-length, khaki shorts and a loose print camp shirt. He was leaning over the counter whispering to the person behind the cash register.

They had planned to browse first and then ask questions, so Molly purposely didn't greet him. Anyway, Stewart looked intent on whatever he was sharing with the seller. Molly and Emma slipped down an aisle. The shop was so tiny it would be difficult for him *not* to see them.

"What's he doing here?" Emma hissed.

Molly shrugged. "Well, he does live in Sarasota."

"Do you think he's selling?"

"Whatever you do, don't accuse him of anything." Molly put her finger to her lips. "Let's just look around."

The shop had a lot of floral and herbal prints, maps, and advertisements from early twentieth-century magazines—hair tonics, radios, shoes, remedies: old ads for "Brylcreem—a Little Dab'll Do Ya," "More Doctors Smoke Camels Than Any Other Cigarette!" The sound of a door closing and the jangle of the bell over the entrance made Molly turn to see Stewart disappear out the door. *Had he seen them?*

At the front desk she asked if there were any illustrations from books, such as fairy tales.

"No, not really. Pretty much everything is out," said the clerk, a young man with bright fire-engine-red hair, spiky on top and shaved on the sides. "That guy who was just here—he sells all sorts of prints. Let me find his card, and I'll give you his contact info."

"That's okay," Molly said. "I know him."

Emma said to the clerk, "Did he sell you anything? Or try to?"

The clerk looked from Molly to Emma and back at Molly. "No-oo. *He* buys from *us*. His prices are too high."

Emma asked, "Did he ask about any book illustrations?"

He straightened up. "What is this?"

Molly said, "Some books were stolen at the Florida Book Fair this weekend, and illustrations were cut out. We're trying to find out what happened to the plates."

"Gawd! How awful. I hope you find them."

Molly pulled out her business card. "If anyone comes in here trying to sell them, could you call me? And the St. Pete police. They're investigating it."

Fire Engine Hair nodded. "Sure will," he said without conviction.

Outside, Emma said, "That was odd. Do you think Stewart told him about the prints?"

Molly crossed her arms. "If so, why did he act as if he didn't know anything?"

Emma shrugged.

"I don't want to suspect Stewart," Molly said. "I like him."

"Well, I'm just asking. It looks suspicious to me."

"Hmmm," Molly said. "So where to next?"

Emma stared at her phone. "Gardenia Street. Très Belle Antique Mall."

"*Très bien.*" Molly had one foot inside her van door and the other on the ground when she looked across the street. "Oh! Over there. Do you see what I see?"

"Thrift store!" Emma exclaimed.

They dashed across the busy street. The thrift store, Fine Finds, had a 60's vintage mannequin in its plate glass window wearing a sleeveless gingham dress, plate-sized shades, and a long chiffon scarf wrapped around her head à la Audrey Hepburn. A vintage pink purse set off her wide skirt and her high-heeled sandals.

Molly and Emma searched the racks. Among the tiny T-shirts with glittery messages in the women's section and the enormous, stiff-as-cardboard long camo-print shorts in the men's, Molly found a new dark blue pair of cropped jeans and three comfortable-looking T-shirts. Black Doc Martens dangled from her other hand.

Emma looked at the Doc Martens. "Really?"

Molly said, "I wore these for most of the Nineties."

Emma was carrying four T-shirts, including a stylish-looking black number with a boat neck and three-quarter-length sleeves, a pink top with short sleeves, a couple of tank tops, and a pair of gray linen cropped pants. She grinned as she piled her finds onto the counter. "With this loot we can stay another week," she said.

"Nooo! I miss Dmitri and Blavatsky," Molly said. "They're my children."

Next, they drove to Très Belle, the antique mall. A former warehouse, it had been festooned with potted plants and vines twisting up around the entrance. They climbed some concrete steps that led to a platform, once used for loading, and walked through a large door into the mall area. A glass counter faced the door, and aisles led away to the left and right. Molly could see glimpses of antique furniture, lamps, and tables laden with smaller items for sale.

A burst of laughter greeted them. Looking directly ahead, Molly saw Eileen Ross on an Art Deco fainting couch. One foot was encased in a medical boot. She was absorbed in talking with Stewart, who was sitting in a plastic chair.

Molly looked at Emma and whispered, "What the—?"

"Molly!" Stewart strode toward them, his face pink. "Are you following me?"

"No!" she exclaimed. "But I do seem to see you everywhere I go."

Stewart said, "I might say the same. At least I have a reason. My booth is here."

Emma said, "Hey, Molly, I'm going to go talk to Eileen about those books."

"Okay." Molly looked at Stewart. "We're trying to find out if anyone—any seller, shop or booth owner—has received those plates that were cut out from the books at the book fair."

"That's exactly what *I'm* doing. I've been going to little shops and booths around here, asking if anyone has had any plates brought in the last couple of days." He gave a small laugh. "I'd like to find the bastards that did it. For one thing, I'd like to clear my name. Some of those book dealers gave me hard looks when I left Sunday. I even heard one say the book fair ought to bar print dealers from now on." He shook his head. "So, you're looking for the prints too? Maybe we should compare notes."

"Sure, I'd like that. Two heads—well, three heads, counting Emma—are better than one. Where's your booth?"

"Over here." Stewart led the way to the back wall where he had a small area surrounded by a couple of tables and a counter. Colorful prints were lined up in display boxes on the sides and against the back wall, with three unpacked boxes in the middle.

"I haven't set up the stuff I took to the fair yet," he said.

"Want some help? I can unpack and you can put them where you want."

"Bless you," he said. "To what do I owe this honor?"

"You can take me and Emma to lunch."

"Emma? Is she um, uh, your uh—?"

"Friend. We're friends." Molly felt her face flush. "She's also from Atlanta." She almost told him about the murder and missing manuscript they investigated last year but decided not to.

"She's cute," Stewart said.

"Yep. Don't get any ideas. She's blessedly single by her own choice."

"When she comes out of her nun-hood, you have first whack, huh?"

"So to speak." Molly grabbed a handful of prints in mylar sleeves and handed them to Stewart. As they worked, each told what they had found out from the print dealers they'd visited.

"All this adds up to very little," said Molly. "Hey, what are these?" She looked at a group of watercolor-looking prints of men with bulging muscles and equally bulging crotches. "That's the Knut guy, right?"

"Oh yeah, Gunnar Knut. I keep his more erotic stuff under the counter." He pulled out a picture of a prince wearing a crown and very little else exposing himself to a young woman who was giving him a coy look, another of two warriors—again leaving little to the imagination—clutching each other, and one, the oddest, that portrayed a group of men of different ethnicities, in various stages of undress, sitting around a small table playing cards in a red room elaborately decorated in Japanese style.

"Well, that's different," Molly said. "I guess they're playing strip poker."

Stewart grinned. "I've known about Knut for years. Chris Kraken had some prints."

"What do you know about Knut? His stuff looks remarkably like Kay Nielsen."

"Umm hmm."

"*Is* he?"

"No one sells them as Kay Nielsens." He stroked his beard. "The story goes that Nielsen was impoverished and started an underground business making art for a specialized audience. Some are straight-up BDSM, gay and straight. A little distasteful for me." He chuckled. "I've kept some for myself, I have to admit." He whispered, "Lesbian!"

"I'd like to see *them*," Molly said. "But not the BDSM."

"Good, clean, woman-on-woman erotica."

Molly smiled. Finally, she and Stewart were talking openly about what they had assumed about each other. It felt good for the barriers to be down.

Chapter 16
Eileen's Story

George MacDonald, The Princess and the Goblin, *Philadelphia: David McKay, 1920. Illustrated by Jessie Willcox Smith. Gray cloth with color illustration pasted down on front cover. Color pictorial endpapers. Ten color illustrations.*

I thought you were from Ohio," Emma said.

"Oh, not anymore," Eileen answered. "We—I—live in Clearwater. We did live in Ohio, but two years ago we moved here to be nearer to our daughter and her family. I grew up in the area and have other family here."

"So did you ever have a brick-and-mortar bookstore?"

"No. Ross Books has always been a traveling show. We used to go to all the book fairs, even New York." Eileen sighed. "It was great fun for years. We liked being peripatetic, sleeping in the van, sometimes on people's floors. We thought we were immortal. But knees and hips started to creak, and sleeping in real beds was better than the back of the van, and we stopped traveling so much. We started selling online in 2000. But we've always set up at the Florida show."

"I'll bet you have some stories," Emma said.

"Oh, yeah." Eileen chuckled. "Like the VW bus we painted to look like a gypsy wagon, all green and pink, with a faux door drawn on the back and a purple morning glory vine twining around it. Jasper had a long beard, and I had black hair to my waist. One time, we were sitting outside in the evening at a KOA campground, and a couple of kids came up and asked if I could tell their fortunes." She laughed. "I actually asked them to cross my palm with silver, and then, when they had dug some dimes out of their wallets, I read their palms. I told them they'd all have long lives and several children."

Emma laughed.

"We went to the Frankfurt Book Fair one summer. I'll never forget it. We didn't have a van, of course; we had Eurail passes. We told ourselves we were just going to look. But we ended up buying a couple of thousand dollars' worth of books on our credit cards and shipping them back home. We thought we were up the creek, but we ended up selling every single book." She gulped. "So many memories. Now it's just me. No one to share them with."

"Do you have any idea who might have done it?" Emma asked in a soft voice.

Eileen's face tightened. "No, I don't. I told the police there's no reason why anyone would want to kill Jasper." She looked down. "I hope they catch the bastard who did it and put them in jail for a long, long time. Jasper didn't deserve to die." Her voice cracked and fell to almost inaudible.

"What about the mutilated books? Do you think there's a connection?"

"How could there be?" Eileen glared.

"I don't mean to trouble you by mentioning it. I'm sorry I said anything."

Eileen looked off into the distance as though she saw more than the glass storefront window of Très Belle and its display of 1950s furniture and Fiesta dishware. Her pale, lined face framed by thick, silver hair, held back with the ever-present barrettes, seemed to look back in time through the window to the washed blue gauze of the sky.

"Are you going to continue selling books?"

"Oh, yes. I'll go on selling online. I don't think I could give it up." Eileen paused. "As soon as all this is over with, we're going to go out into the bay and scatter Jasper's ashes. He always loved it here. We'll go at dawn. I guess I'll read something from Winnie the Pooh. Or maybe Alan Ginsberg."

"Those don't seem to have much in common."

"To Jasper they did," said Eileen. A hint of a smile lifted the corners of her mouth. Emma saw her for a moment as the adventurous girl she had once been, all flowing hair and bright print scarves, face not classically beautiful but alight with life.

Emma hesitated. Did what she was about to ask sound crass? "Um, Eileen, you know those books Jasper took from me to show to you, the ones that disappeared?"

"Oh, yeah. You said he wanted to buy them from you."

"Well, all but one of them has turned up. People have returned them. It seems Jasper left them in different booths."

"I knew he wasn't up to doing the book fair anymore."

"Well—I was wondering whether—you're still interested."

"Remind me again—what are they?"

"*Alice in Wonderland* illustrated by Ralph Steadman, *The Little Prince, And to Think That I Saw It—*"

"*On Mulberry Street,*" they said in unison, Eileen smiling. "White shorts?" she asked.

"Yes, the true first edition. And *A Child's Garden of Verses* illustrated by Jessie Willcox Smith."

"Condition?"

"They're all in very good to fine condition. *The Little Prince* has some minor chips on the dust jacket, and there's a previous owner's name on the front free endpaper of *Mulberry Street*."

"Prices?"

"I'll have to double-check, but Jasper said he thought they were quite reasonable. I'll bring them here and you can look at them."

"Please do. And if I'm not here, Sus—ah, Stewart can keep them for me in his booth."

"How long have you known Stewart?" Emma asked.

"I'm his aunt! His mother is my sister." Eileen looked amused at Emma's astonishment. "You know, I wasn't surprised with the change. Susan was always more like a little boy than a little girl. It's just like that sometimes." She shifted in her seat. "I'm going to have to go in a minute," she said. "This boot is a damn nuisance."

◈◈◈

Emma sat with Molly and Stewart in a semi-enclosed patio, digging into their lunches. Emma munched happily on a large, leafy, green salad with tomatoes and avocado, while Molly attacked her veggie taco. Stewart was enjoying a burrito after adding some hot sauce. He offered the plastic bottle to Molly.

"No, thanks." Molly waved it away. "I don't like anything that's too hot."

"I love the heat," said Stewart, mouth full. "Tex-Mex is my favorite."

After they had finished eating and the waiter took away their plates, Emma pulled out her note pad and pen. "So, shall we share what we've learned so far?"

"Okay," Molly said, "although it doesn't add up to much."

"First," said Emma, "Jasper was found dead in the parking lot behind the Flying Dutchman."

"Jasper was dead, to begin with," Molly quipped.

Emma shot Molly a frown.

Molly's face turned pink. "Sorry. Dickens, *A Christmas Carol*, first line."

Emma continued, "And someone stole some books from the booths at the fair on Friday and Saturday and returned them on Sunday morning with the illustrations cut out."

"Question." Molly raised her index finger. "Did anyone look at the boxes the books were returned in? Is there anything interesting about them?"

"Actually, I did," Emma said. "I noticed that they were new banker's boxes, plain. They looked as though someone might have just bought them, and they had 'Returned Books' written on them."

"Good!" Molly said. "Is there an Office Depot or a Staples near the Coliseum? If not, where's the nearest one?"

Stewart tapped his phone. "Office Depot on Thirty-seventh Street. But they probably won't tell us anything about who bought the boxes."

"We have to start somewhere," Emma said. "But Office Depot boxes usually have their name on them. And these were blank except for the hand lettering."

Molly said, "I noticed an office supply store just off Central Avenue. I could ask there."

Emma asked, "And where are those boxes anyway?"

"Kitty takes anything away from the Coliseum that's left behind. I imagine she would keep them to use. Booksellers don't throw away boxes." Molly thought briefly of her own house, where boxes were stacked up in any free corner. She was always meaning to break them down and stow them in closets.

Emma said, "Oh, I forgot to tell you—Eileen might buy all four books from me!"

"Yay!" Molly raised her iced tea in Emma's direction. They all clinked glasses.

"And she wants me to bring the books to Très Belle. Can we do that tomorrow?"

"Of course. I am so glad you're going to sell those books!"

"Yes, good news!" Stewart grinned.

Chapter 17
Boxes

Rachel Field, Hitty: Her First Hundred Years, *New York: Macmillan, 1929. First edition. Illustrated by Dorothy P. Lathrop. Patterned cloth boards with pictorial paper title label on front cover. Illustrated dust jacket. The classic story of a doll and her numerous owners. Full page and partial page black and white plates as well as three color plates. Won the Newbery Medal for 1930.*

A bell tinkled when Molly entered Ford's Office Supply. The shelves were packed with all sorts of useful items and stacks of paper. Nothing appeared to have been dusted recently. A middle-aged man and woman were behind the counter. From their body language, Molly was afraid she was interrupting a personal conversation. One of those metal bells used to summon hotel clerks sat on the counter, along with scissors, tape dispensers, pencil sharpeners, pencils, and ball point pens with "Ford's Your One-Stop Supply Store" imprinted on them.

"Hi," Molly said. She wondered whether she ought to buy something before asking questions and decided it might be a good idea. "Do you have a ruler that has the metric system as well as inches?"

The woman smiled, red lipstick on her teeth matching her lips. "Right over there." She pointed to the far corner. She wore a floral sleeveless blouse and several bangles on her wrist.

"Thanks." Molly found a blue Lucite ruler and took it to the counter. The man was using a box cutter on a large rectangular package. The woman rang her up and thanked her for her business.

"By the way, do you sell banker's boxes?"

The man answered, "Sure. We carry two sizes. You gotta put 'em together yourself."

"That's fine. Um. I was wondering…did anyone buy any on Saturday?"

"Why are you asking?"

Molly told them about the books being stolen and returned. "In four new boxes."

"Oh my!" The woman said. "I didn't sell the boxes myself, but I do remember seeing the sale on the computer when I closed out on Saturday. Let me double check." She clicked her mouse a few times, and called out, "L.T.!"

"What?" came a peeved-sounding voice.

"Come'ere!" she shouted.

A teen-aged boy trudged to the front. An orange T-shirt hung loosely on him, the chest pocket stretched out of shape. His jeans hung low beneath his belly.

"You sold that order of four boxes, didn't you? On Saturday."

"Uh, yeah," L.T. said. "What about it? I didn't do nothin' wrong, did I?" He shoved his hands into his back pocket.

"Stand up straight, son," the woman shopkeeper said.

Molly asked, "Do you remember who bought them?"

"No. Nobody I know."

"Do you remember what they looked like?"

He looked Molly up and down. He was probably wondering if he had to answer her.

"I'm not the police," she said. "Some books were stolen, defaced, and returned in new-looking boxes. We're trying to figure out who did it."

"Just some guy, kinda dark-looking." He straightened up. "I remember the car, a long one with doors that open toward each other."

Molly chuckled. "They used to call them suicide doors."

"I asked him what kind of car it was, and he said a Lincoln Continental. Nineteen-sixty-something."

Molly froze. An old Lincoln had been in the parking lot at Kitty's shop on Monday.

"It was pretty, too. Light blue with a black top. A lady was driving it."

A lady? A suspicion wormed its way into Molly's mind. "What did she look like?"

"She was old, but kind of pretty. Black hair, wearing something red."

Carmen? "Thanks, L.T." Molly rushed to the door, but the woman called out, "Don't forget your ruler!"

With the ruler in hand, Molly almost ran to the van. She had to get right over to Sandpiper Books. And call Emma and Stewart.

∽∾

The parking lot was mostly empty when Molly arrived at Sandpiper Books. Only a black Toyota that was probably Kitty's. Inside the store, Kitty was sitting behind the counter staring intently at her phone. She glanced up and went back to tapping. "Just a sec, Molly. I'm finishing a game and can't stop. The slime is going to cover the frogs." She groaned and set the phone down. "Lost again." Then she smiled her book fair publicist smile. "What's up?"

"I was wondering if you drive a Lincoln Continental?"

"What? On a bookseller's meager profits?"

"When we came in Monday night, there was an old Lincoln, like from the sixties, blue with a black top, with those doors that open from the middle."

"Really? They had doors like that?"

Of course, Kitty was a good bit younger than herself. "I was hoping you knew who it belonged to."

"Why?"

"That's my other question. You know I'm still sick over those defaced books." Molly frowned. "Emma said they arrived on the Coliseum steps in brand new banker's boxes. So, I went to that office supply place on Central, and they said four boxes were bought there. The person who bought them loaded them into a Lincoln like I described. I wondered if maybe you saw who was driving it."

"No, I didn't. The parking lot is around back, and when I'm behind the counter, I'm facing away from the driveway, so I have no way of knowing who drives what."

"Do you still have those boxes the books were in?"

Kitty shook her head. "The cops asked about the boxes first thing and took them for evidence. Since Emma and I both had handled them, they said they might not be able to get fingerprints, but they'd try. Same with the books—they would have been handled by lots of people."

"Well, thanks, anyway. You can go back to fighting slime monsters."

ↄ⌇ↄ

After dinner and a mojito, Molly was feeling relaxed. She and Emma were both sitting in their own beds, propped on the extra pillows. Molly was reading the latest *Rizzoli and Isles* mystery but had to keep closing her eyes to rest them and then hunt for where she had left off reading. This happened a few times. When Rizzoli started peering into some empty cardboard boxes, and Isles drove up in a light blue Lincoln Continental filled with books, Molly gave up trying to stay awake. She put the mystery novel on the bedside table and turned off the light over her bed.

"Calling it a night?" Emma asked. She held her book closer to her eyes.

"Yep." Although Molly had thought she was going to drop off to sleep, now that the light was out, her mind kept whirring. She tried to remember how many people were in Sandpiper Books on Monday. Carmen…she didn't want to think about her. But she felt something was unfinished with Emma. "Emma?"

"Yeah?" Emma sounded drowsy. "I'm trying to finish my chapter."

"Okay."

There was Carmen and the woman who returned the books. It seemed there were more people in the bookstore. A heavy-set man was putting books on the counter at Kitty's last call, but Molly hadn't thought much about checking anybody out. She was still stunned at having seen Carmen and at how she had acted like they were old friends.

"Okay, I'm done," Emma said. "I'll be right back."

While Emma was in the bathroom, Molly's mind kept returning to Monday night. And try as she might, she couldn't remember whether the Lincoln was in the lot behind Sandpiper Books when they had left.

Emma climbed in bed and turned off the light, and Molly felt as though she could finally talk to her friend about Carmen. "Emma, I've been going over and over in my mind who was at Sandpiper Books that night. But every time, it starts with Carmen."

"Umm?"

"I think I'm ready to tell you about her."

"It's okay," Emma said. "I was out of line."

"I'm ready." Molly breathed in deeply, exhaled, and began. "Carmen and I met five years ago. The book fair had just ended, and I was sitting at the bar at the Central Avenue Seafood Shack. The music was a tape of old eighties songs. I was humming along to 'Girls Just Wanna Have Fun,' when this woman leaned over and said, 'One of your favorites?' and I said, 'God, I used to dance to this.' Then every song that came on, we'd see who was the first to have the title. I'm awful at song names, I just remember the tune and some of the lyrics." Molly wadded up one of the pillows and held it tight against her chest. "Long story short, I ended up going home with her. Come to find out, she sold cocaine. And it was pure before she cut it. We did a lot of cocaine. And had sex. Lots of sex."

She was glad the lights were off. "It was a time in my life when I was experimenting a lot with drugs. I'd get together with other book dealers and antique dealers and smoke."

Emma said nothing. Molly could feel her listening. She sighed and continued. "Anyway, Carmen and I did cocaine and had sex for almost a week. And in between, people were coming over to buy, and so we'd snort some with them. We'd call for takeout—Chinese, Greek, pizza, submarines, you name it." She sensed that Emma was very still. Molly turned on her side facing Emma. "You still awake?"

"Go on."

Molly pressed on. "Finally, I told Carmen that I had to get back to my life, but that she was welcome to come visit me in Atlanta sometime. I headed to my mother's for a day or two. Early in the morning after I got there, my mother came to the bedroom where I was staying, and Carmen was with her. Mama left to go to work, and Carmen came into my bed, but it was already different, as if I had been under a spell at her house. It was creepy that she just showed up there like a stalker. I asked her how she found my mother's house, and she said she figured it out from my description. I got up, and we went to visit the Marjorie Kinnan Rawlings house. When we got back, I asked her to leave. I didn't want her there. I was visiting Mama." She paused.

Emma said, "I'm still listening."

"A couple days later, I was at home getting ready to deposit my money from the book fair, and somehow the numbers weren't coming out right. I had added up my sales on Sunday and counted the money in my pouch. But when I counted my cash at home, I was two hundred and fifty dollars short. I used to get paid in cash at the book fair. Now people mostly use their credit or debit cards. I had kept the pouch with me, and I paid for the pizza delivery out of it once, but usually either Carmen paid out of her cocaine money, or I used my debit card. I like to keep my book money separate, except I sometimes use it for meals while traveling on business. Anyway, I knew I hadn't spent two hundred and fifty. This was so long ago that I didn't use my cell phone much, but Carmen had my home number in Atlanta. She had called me three times and left messages before I even got home. I didn't call her back. I couldn't prove she had taken the money, but I just had a hunch." Molly squeezed the pillow tighter. "So, I decided, if she called again, not to answer the phone.

"But she kept calling. She'd call at least twice a day, leaving messages asking where I was. I was so sick of it that one day I answered the phone, and it was her. She started crying and saying she was so worried that something horrible had happened to me. I said, 'Something horrible *has* happened. You stole from me.' She said, 'Well, you and I used a lot of product that I'll never be able to sell, and I owe this guy.' And I said, 'If you wanted me to pay for what we were snorting, all you had to do was ask. Quit calling me.' After a few weeks she called again and asked if I was still mad. I told her that everything that happened was a bad mistake and to not call again or come to my booth in Florida. I said I didn't want to see her again."

"You haven't talked to her or seen her since?"

"Not until Monday. God!" Molly put the pillow on her face. "What you must think of me."

Emma was quiet a moment. "What I think is—well, sometimes it's easy to get caught up in someone's orbit."

"Yeah." An overwhelming sense of relief washed over Molly. Emma wasn't judging her, just listening. She sat up. "Oh my god, I just remembered! Carmen drove this 1960s Thunderbird. Her father and brother restored classic cars."

"What does that have to do with—?"

"I bet that Lincoln is hers! Just the kinda car she would drive. What was she doing picking up those boxes?"

"Do you think *she's* the one who returned the books?"

"Maybe." Molly said slowly. Sleep seemed far away now. She'd had enough sleepless nights going over what happened with Carmen, but now, was Carmen in the middle of this theft? And perhaps the murder as well?

Chapter 18
Decisions

Louisa May Alcott, Eight Cousins, or, the Aunt-Hill. *Boston: Roberts Brothers, 1875. First edition. Blue cloth with gilt decoration and lettering on spine. Black and white frontispiece with tissue guard, illustrated in black and white throughout.*

The next morning, Emma came back to the room after breakfast to find Molly up, dressed, and bent over her phone.

"I thought you'd still be asleep. I would have waited for you," Emma said. "But I know you like to sleep later than I do."

"That's okay." Molly looked up and smiled. "You look great in that pink top."

Emma felt her face flush. "It's one of my thrift shop finds." She hadn't tried it on in the shop. When she got dressed this morning, she discovered that the heart-shaped neckline was lower than she had thought.

"I like it." Molly kept looking at her.

Emma felt prompted to say something. "So, have you found anything?" She didn't want to say, *Have you found Carmen?*

Molly nodded. "I found Carmen on Facebook. She has

pictures of herself with this guy at the beach. Then a group of people standing around a fancy antique car show. I was just wondering whether to friend her or not. I'd see more information that way, but she'd get access to my information. And that might open up a whole can of worms."

Emma sat beside her. "It sure would. I don't know. I don't think it's a good idea for you to get involved with her again." She didn't like how the word "involved" sounded and added quickly, "I mean, not after what she did. She sounds like trouble."

"Oh, she is. No doubt about that." Molly put down the phone. "But I may have to."

"What?" Emma sounded more horrified than she meant to.

"Oh, I don't mean get *involved* with her!" Molly said quickly. "But I think she may be key to what happened to the books. I'll bet that car is hers, and I think I need to find her and ask her some questions."

Emma felt a rush of anxiety. The woman *was* attractive: sexy in an open, out-there kind of way. "Do you—*want* to see her?"

"No! If it was up to me, I'd never lay eyes on her again. Not after what she did." Molly's jaw set. "But we said we'd investigate and find out what happened. That's what we're doing."

"Are you sure?" Emma said.

"Emma," Molly shook her head. "I'm as interested in getting together again with Carmen as I am in getting a serious case of poison ivy. With hives thrown in. And sunburn. And seventeen kinds of mosquitoes all biting me at once."

Emma smiled. When Molly laughed, she joined in. "Okay, I believe you."

"Do you?" Molly turned to face her. "Because—what you think of me is important."

Emma nodded, wordless. Molly's leg against her made Emma's face flush. She touched it with her cool hand.

"I made some mistakes and Carmen was one of them. And drugs. But I never got in deep. I was lucky, I guess."

Emma said, "You're full of surprises, you know. I had no idea you had been involved in the drug culture so much."

"It was just for a short while. But I have smoked a lot of pot. I don't do any of that now. Does it bother you?"

"A little." Emma struggled for words. "You're not quite who I thought you were."

"Is anybody?"

"No. I guess not."

"I'm actually not sorry about most of the things I did. I've learned a lot. About people, about myself."

"You learned how to take care of yourself," Emma said. When Molly nodded, Emma added, "and you learned how to get out of situations, how to break away."

Molly said, "Yes, I wish I had known how to do that earlier." She ran her hand through her short hair. "As you know, I stayed too long with my last partner."

Emma said quietly, "I did too. It's much easier to get into a relationship than to get out of one."

They looked at one another again. After a moment, Molly said, "So what's our next move?"

"I think you should friend Carmen on Facebook. Find out if she still lives in the same place, and then we both—" She spoke firmly. "We *both* will go and talk to her."

Molly gave her a quick grin. "Sounds like a plan. Hey, I'm going to get a coffee and something, I don't know, a croissant. Want to go with?"

"Sure."

Chapter 19
Venus Flytrap

E.B. White, Charlotte's Web, New York: Harper and Brothers, 1952. Illustrated by Garth Williams. First edition with code "I-B" on copyright page. Cloth, pictorial dust jacket. Blue and white spider-web patterned endpapers. Line drawing illustrations throughout. Newbery Honor Book for 1953.

Sitting with Emma at a table in the hotel restaurant, Molly proceeded to add Carmen as a friend on Facebook, Snapchat, Twitter, and Instagram. She had hardly had time to get her coffee creamed and sugared the way she liked it when she got a message: "Hey, Mol, it was great seeing you the other day! Are you still in town?"

"Yep," Molly wrote on her keypad, holding it between herself and Emma so that her friend could see. "How ya doing? Are you still in the same house?"

"Yes. (Smiley face) How much longer will you be here?"

"Few days."

"Stop by when you get a chance. You know me, I'm always at home."

Molly set her phone on the table. She took a bite of

bacon and blueberry pancakes. She had intended to order only coffee and a muffin but couldn't resist the special.

Emma sat back, sipped her tea, and raised an eyebrow.

"Carmen's always home. That's what she said when people called, so I'm sure that means she's still dealing."

Emma asked, "Are we going over there?"

"I'm gonna tell her I might stop by."

"By yourself?" Emma arched an eyebrow.

"Nooo. I'll just say 'I' because I don't want her to think anything is up."

"Ha! When she sees me, that'll burst her bubble."

"I'm really glad you're going. I don't think I'd have the nerve by myself."

Emma placed her hand on Molly's. "I'll keep you from being seduced," she said in a sultry tone.

"Thank you, Lauren Bacall," Molly said.

"Remember, she stalked you."

Molly nodded. To lighten things up, she winked at Emma. "She might try to seduce *you*. Especially in that pink top. I should've said you were my girlfriend when she asked."

Emma blushed.

Molly smiled to herself and scooped up a blueberry with a forkful of pancake.

∽∾

Molly pulled her van into a gravel driveway in front of a stucco bungalow from the 1920's, probably built around the same time as the Coliseum. The blue Lincoln was in the driveway, and a pick-up was parked behind it. Molly let out her breath in a great gust. She didn't look forward to this. What had been a whirlwind romance had turned into Tropical Storm Carmen. But tropical storms eventually die out. They don't return.

"I'll be right here with you." Emma patted her shoulder.

"Thank goodness," Molly said.

They rang the bell and the door opened, revealing Carmen in a long orange caftan with a canna lily print. Each lily stretched the length of the caftan. Her dark hair was swept up with a few wavy strands falling around her face. She was barefoot, and her toenails were orange with glitter. Even without shoes she was nearly six feet tall. She threw her arms around Molly, and Molly recognized the strong, sweet scent of Carmen's favorite cologne. She cringed inside at what she imagined Emma must be thinking. Glitter? Cologne at eleven a.m.?

Molly stepped out of the embrace and introduced Emma.

Carmen looked Emma up and down. "Sit, sit," she said, waving toward the coffee table. A Latin man wearing a black Tampa Bay Rays cap sprawled in a recliner next to a long sofa checking his phone.

"This is my cousin, Luis," Carmen said, sitting on the sofa. Luis looked up from the phone and nodded. He and Carmen exchanged a few words in Spanish, and then he left. Molly heard his truck roar away. Emma headed to the chair he had vacated. Molly settled in at the corner of the couch. She glanced at the TV, tuned to CNN. She looked down at the coffee table, where she saw a mirror and a rolled-up dollar bill. Nope, Carmen hadn't changed.

Carmen smiled and put her hand on Molly's knee. "Look, Molly, I'm sorry how things turned out before. We can be friends?"

"Sure. It's been a long time." She didn't forgive her, and Carmen hadn't asked for forgiveness. And to be honest, no, Molly didn't want to be friends. She wanted information. "Hey, I like the Lincoln. That yours?"

"Yeah, it's cherry, isn't it?"

"Sure is," Emma said. "I've never seen doors that open

that way."

"Suicide doors, they call them. But I don't know them to be more dangerous than other doors."

Molly said, "Bet there aren't too many like that around."

"That's for sure." Carmen turned to Emma. "So, Emma, you're a bookseller, too?"

Emma nodded. "I am. Clarke's Collectibles is my business name. I sell mostly children's and illustrated books."

"Oh, my favorites!" Carmen exclaimed. "Do you...partake?" She waved a baggy with white powder in Emma's direction.

"Oh, no," Emma said quickly.

"Me neither," Molly said.

"Your loss." Carmen shrugged and leaned toward Molly. "You used to love it so."

"That was then."

"Now, don't let what happened before..."

Molly interrupted. "I don't really do any drugs, now, not even pot."

"Okay, okay. You don't mind...?"

"Go right ahead." Molly felt a twinge of annoyance. Carmen had changed the subject just when she was getting started talking about the Lincoln.

As Carmen bent over the mirror, using a razor blade to chop up the cocaine, Emma caught Molly's eye. *Well, Emma had known what to expect*, Molly thought.

Molly decided to take charge of the conversation. "So, Carmen, when you were in Kitty's bookstore, did you happen to see someone come in with some books that she said she found in her booth at the Coliseum?"

Carmen grunted, focused on the powder and razor blade. She picked up the dollar bill on the table, rolled it tighter, and snorted the powder into one nostril. She put her paraphernalia on the coffee table and sat back. "Now what?"

"Did you notice anyone come in with some books?" Molly tried to keep her voice patient.

Carmen raised her head and brushed a wavy strand of dark hair out of her eyes. "What?" She sounded accusing to Molly, not as though she didn't understand.

"Someone brought some books into Sandpiper Books." Molly spoke slowly. "A woman. She said she found them in her booth. I wondered if you were there when she came in."

"I don't remember seeing anyone come in—except you all. Who's Kitty?"

"She owns the bookstore. She was wearing a flowered sundress."

"Hey, anybody want some coffee? I'll go make some." Carmen jumped up, caftan swirling around her.

"Ah, yeah, coffee would be fine," Molly said with a sigh. She shrugged.

Carmen disappeared into the kitchen. Molly could hear her humming and setting up the coffeemaker.

Molly called, "So did you hear about what happened at the Colis—?"

"Sorry, I can't hear you," Carmen called. Molly heard more kitchen noises and a muttered "Shit!" as something that sounded like plastic rattled on the counter.

Carmen whisked back into the room and took her seat. "Now what were you saying?"

"I was asking if you heard about what happened at the Coliseum this past weekend."

"No, what?"

"A man was killed. A book dealer. He was found dead in the parking lot of a hotel near the Coliseum."

"I heard that on the news." Carmen's face looked sympathetic. "Did you know him?"

"Yeah, I've known him a long time." She thought, *I don't want to admit that it was Emma and I who found him.*

"And some books were stolen and brought back on Sunday, defaced. The illustrations were cut out."

"How awful!" Carmen's bare foot jiggled, and she clasped and unclasped her hands.

Molly continued. "We—Emma and I—are trying to find out who did it."

Carmen's foot stopped jiggling.

Molly leaned forward. "I'm hoping you can help us. The books are important—they are people's livelihoods. And the man who was killed was carrying some of Emma's books, and one is still missing."

Carmen leapt to her feet. "Coffee's ready."

Molly and Emma waited as Carmen brought in a tray with three cups of coffee, silver spoons, a small artisan ceramic cream pitcher, and a matching sugar bowl.

"Cream? Sugar?" Carmen asked. "I don't have any artificial stuff. I like the real thing." She laughed as she handed the cups around and sat down.

Molly and Emma fixed their coffees and sipped. The thick cream and raw sugar enhanced Molly's enjoyment.

"So—," Molly began, but Carmen sprang out of her seat again.

"I have some cookies," she said. "Anybody want any?"

Emma shook her head vigorously.

Molly said, "No, thanks. We just had breakfast. We wanted to ask you—"

"Yeah," Carmen perched on the edge of the sofa, knees touching Molly's. "I just don't know what to tell you. I went in the bookstore to get a present for my little niece. She loves princesses, so I wanted to get a Disney princess book for her. I was looking around in the kids' section when I saw you." She smiled at Molly, a smile that made its way into her voice, sweetening it. "You haven't changed a bit."

Molly said, "Thanks." She wondered whether that was

a compliment. She noticed that Emma kept her eyes on her coffee cup as she sipped.

"You're looking well, Carmen. Nice. You look nice." Molly decided to use a little honey to get what she wanted.

"Thank you!"

Molly tried again. "Several booksellers had their books cut up, the illustrations cut out. Some won't ever be able to recover their losses. If we can find out who or what is behind this, it would make a big difference to a lot of people."

Carmen nodded. At that moment, the cellphone on the table beside her buzzed, and she picked it up. "Hi," she said. "Yeah, sure, come on over. I'm at home. I'll be here all day. Okay, see you in a bit." She ended the call and placed the phone down within easy reach.

"Funny thing is," Molly continued, "the books were returned in four brand new banker's boxes with the plates cut out. Just left on the steps outside."

"Mmhmm," Carmen said.

"So, we were trying to find out who bought the boxes. You didn't happen to buy any lately, did you?"

"Mo-ll-y," Carmen said, stretching out her name.

"We're trying to track down who defaced those books."

"You think *I* would cut up *books*?" Carmen's eyes pierced Molly's.

"Of course not." Molly tried to sound soothing. "We were just trying to follow through on a tip that a lady in a Lincoln bought some boxes from Ford's on Saturday."

"Yes, I did get some boxes there. My brother and his family are moving, and I helped them wrap up the dishes and stuff."

"Okay, okay," Molly said. "Sorry I asked."

Carmen continued glaring at Molly, and then looked over at Emma, who was gazing intently at an oil painting across from the recliner.

"You like that painting?"

Emma said, "Yes. You have some really nice art." The canvas pictured a woman in a white nightdress standing on a balcony wringing out a red-stained sheet over the iron rail. The red streaks blended into the red of a sunset.

"I collect art by women," Carmen said. "That's a Leonora Carrington."

Emma's eyes widened. "An original?"

Carmen gave a half smile. "I came into some money a few years back, and I got it at auction. Pretty lucky, huh?" She leaned back. "Carrington's kind of disturbing, actually. That's one of her more normal-looking pieces."

Wonder where the money came from? Molly thought.

"Years ago, I went to the National Museum of Women in the Arts in DC," Carmen gestured toward another wall. "I got that Remedios Varo poster. Isn't it great?"

Molly looked at the framed poster. A woman in a khaki trench coat and a bowler hat was steering a boat through a swamp, a boat made from her own hat that curved around and under her. "Oh, my goodness," Molly said. "That's amazing."

Carmen chuckled. "Yes, isn't it? I like Remedios even better than Frida Kahlo. She's so out there, such a visionary."

Molly drew her eyes from the poster. "Well, I think we'd better go."

"Oh, don't hurry off!" Carmen exclaimed. "Would you like to see my garden? I've got a real Venus flytrap!"

"Maybe another time," Molly said.

"Okay. It's been so good to see you. We'll have to get together real soon and catch up." Carmen stood as Molly did and enveloped her in a hug.

"So nice to meet you," she said to Emma, smiling like a cat with cream on its whiskers.

Molly and Emma didn't speak until they were back in the car and zipping along the street that led away from

Carmen's.

"Well!" Emma said. "You're still obviously under her spell."

"What?!" Molly burst out.

"You just accepted her lame excuse about the boxes without even asking a question. I thought we went there to find some real information!"

"I did ask questions," Molly said. She swung the car around a corner with more force than she meant to.

"But when she gave you that story about helping her brother move and getting the boxes to pack up dishes and stuff, you just backed off."

"Well, what would you have done?" Molly snapped. "You don't know what she's like. If she doesn't want to tell you something, she won't."

"That was mildly obvious," Emma answered. "I can see how you had a hard time getting away from *her*. Art, coffee with real cream and sugar, and all the rest—" She made her voice fake sweet. "She's a real charmer—wearing cologne at eleven o'clock in the morning."

"Maybe so, but it didn't work, did it?"

"Didn't it? She didn't give out any information."

"Emma." Molly gritted her teeth. "What should I have said?" Emma was right, she thought. *Have I been sucked in once more by Carmen's charms?*

"For starters, why didn't you push her about the boxes?"

"Emma, I couldn't just accuse her of lying right then and there!"

Emma crossed her arms and looked out the window.

Molly suddenly thought of something. "Anyway, why didn't *you* ask those questions? You were sitting right there. But *you* started talking about art."

It was Emma's turn to look uncomfortable. "Well," she began, uncrossing her arms. "I don't know her. I..."

"See!" Molly said. "You didn't have the nerve either.

Or were *you* under her spell?"

"Okay, okay." Emma threw up her hands. "Neither of us is quite the investigative hotshot we might like to be. I admit, I can be cowed sometimes."

Molly was quiet. Emma had thrown her off guard by frankly admitting a mistake or a weakness. "All right," she said. "Let's be more careful in the future not to be taken in by people we're questioning."

"That's okay," Emma said. "I know it was difficult to see her again. You actually managed it quite well." She gave a rueful smile. "I know a little myself about those Venus flytraps."

Chapter 20
Bridges

Coussens, Penrhyn W., ed., A Child's Book of Stories, New York: Duffield & Co., 1911. First edition. Dark blue cloth with gilt lettering on front and spine, color illustration pasted on front. Illustrated by Jessie Willcox Smith. Pictorial endpapers, full color frontispiece with tissue guard. Stories from: Arabian Nights, Aesop, Charles Perrault, Grimm, Andersen, English Folktales, and Myths. Ten full page illustrations.

I sure hope Eileen buys these books," Emma said, patting the tote bag at her feet. "I'll be so glad to finally sell them."

She and Molly were in Molly's van, headed for Sarasota after leaving Carmen's.

"I know. We should be able to get there before two o'clock." Molly turned out of the old St. Pete neighborhood toward I-275. "And let's check in with Stewart. Maybe he'll be at the antique mall."

Emma's phone showed 117 unread emails. They tended to stack up when she wasn't home to delete the clothing sales, left-wing alarmist petitions, and hot Russian women waiting to meet *her*. She dialed Eileen's number and got voice mail. She called Stewart.

"Hey, what's up?" he asked.

"We're on the way to Très Belle. You know, Eileen said to bring the books to your booth, so we wanted to know if you were there."

"I'm at home. Why don't y'all stop by here for lunch?"

"I told Eileen—"

Emma heard Stewart take a deep breath. "Listen, Aunt Eileen's afraid to leave the house. And she's not answering the phone. I told her I'd take her the books. So come on over here. I'd love to make lunch for you two. You driving?"

"Molly is."

"Okay, tell me when you're ready for my address."

She balanced her notepad on her knees while listening. She had never quite gotten the hang of doing multiple tasks on her phone. After ending the call, she said, "Change of plans, Mol, we're going to Stewart's for lunch. He insisted."

Emma was glad Molly was driving. It would be nice, she thought, if the two of them could pack all their books into Molly's van and drive to St. Pete together next year. When the van sped up and Molly merged onto I-275 South, zipping between a truck and a van, Emma grabbed her shoulder belt. As Molly picked up speed and slid in right behind a car in the fast lane, Emma's foot pressed down on the floor. That imaginary passenger side brake was one she often found herself stomping when riding with someone who drove faster than she did. To distract herself, she relayed Stewart's conversation.

Molly frowned. "Eileen seemed in a good mood when we saw her at Très Belle."

"Well, maybe not exactly good. Wistful, maybe." Emma searched for the right word. "Nostalgic about their adventures."

"I wonder what made her afraid," Molly said. "You think she's frightened that the murderer will come after her?"

"I hope not. I've been wondering if it was a random killing." At Molly's questioning glance, Emma said, "You know, maybe Jasper was in the wrong place at the wrong time."

The road curved, and Emma saw the highest part of the bridge looming ahead. An ominous sign warned motorists, "Next Fuel Stop 20 Miles." She felt the van shift into a lower gear as the bridge rose in front of them.

"Molly, please get in the middle lane." Emma hated traveling at high speed, and she suddenly was aware of how close to the edge the van was.

Molly swung over to the next lane. On the first trip over the bridge, Molly had pointed out pilings from the old bridge, still standing. She'd explained that the old bridge collapsed in the eighties and that the new, higher bridge had replaced it.

Emma held her breath and clung to the seat belt. "Molly," she said. "Don't you think you're awfully close to that car—ahh!" she shrieked as Molly zipped around the car in front of them.

"It doesn't help when you do that."

"Didn't mean to. My gasp was involuntary." Maybe it wouldn't be such a good idea after all for them to travel to St. Pete together in one van. She watched as the tailgate of the Kia Soul in front of them got closer and closer. Molly still hadn't braked. Emma's jaw tightened.

As the end of the bridge came in sight, Emma said, "Hey, Molly. Do you still think Carmen is involved with those books that were defaced?"

Molly answered slowly, "I don't know...I mean, she *was* mad when I asked her about the boxes, but she so quickly said what they were used for."

"She *said* she was helping her brother move. You ever meet him? Does she have more than one?"

"The brother was the baby in a family of six girls."

"Six? Wow."

"Right! I met the brother once. His name's Manny. He dropped by Carmen's house the week I stayed with her." She looked away from Emma's side-eyed glance.

"Could you go check with her brother to see if he moved recently?"

A wide grin crossed Molly's face. "Now you're thinking like a detective."

"All those years of being a critical reader."

ↄ∫ↄ∫

Stewart met them at the door wearing a loose blue T-shirt and cut-off jeans. "Come in, come in." The house was small with an eclectic mix of antiques, Ikea, and thrift-shop modern. A long brick-and-board bookshelf held books and stacks of what appeared to be matted prints. On a small mahogany knick-knack shelf, Emma noticed a square milk glass candy dish. "I like your candy dish. My mother had one just like it," she said to Stewart.

"I collect old glass serving dishes," he said. He ushered them through the living room into a tiny dining room with an old oak table set with three woven placemats and stainless cutlery. "Have a seat. I made some Raspberry Zinger iced tea. Or I can make coffee."

"Zinger suits me," Emma said.

Molly said, "Me too."

Emma glanced around the dining room. Its windows had no curtains but were hung with baskets of variegated philodendron plants that draped their foliage to the windowsills. She wrinkled her nose with pleasure: the enticing smell of bacon, along with garlic, dill, and other herbs wafted from the kitchen.

Emma sat down at one of the three place settings and put the canvas bag containing Eileen's books on a chair.

Molly sat across from Emma in front of a green soup tureen that looked like a turtle, filled with a pale green, creamy soup garnished with bits of dill.

"I'm so glad you called when you did," Stewart carried in two ice-filled red drinks. "I made this chilled cucumber soup, and I was afraid I'd have to eat it every day this week." He left and came back with a large yellow bowl that Emma recognized as part of a set that was in every 1960's household. "Hot German potato salad. I wasn't sure if y'all ate meat, so the bacon is on the side."

"Great," Molly said. "Hot potato salad and cold soup!"

"So here are the books," Emma said, gesturing toward the bag.

"Thanks for bringing them. I don't know what's up with Aunt Eileen, but I'm going to see her later. Maybe I'll find out what's got her worried."

Stewart served soup into bowls and spooned potato salad onto china plates. "Dig in."

Emma dipped her spoon into her soup, making sure one of the wisps of dill was included. A perfect melding of tastes. "Mmm." She crumbled a strip of bacon onto the potato salad.

"Also," Stewart said, "I wanted to tell you about my conversation with Office Mart. I was referred from one person to another and finally I was taken to the store manager. He wouldn't tell me anything and said the police had already been there." Stewart stopped to sprinkle bacon on his own potato salad and blushed. "So—I have to admit I lied a little. Well, I lied a lot. I said I was working undercover on the case and hinted that it involved more than books. And it got worse. He asked to see my badge, and I explained that I couldn't carry any ID because if I were intercepted, it couldn't be known that I was a cop."

"Good thinking," Emma said.

"I'm impressed," Molly said. "Not only by your lie, but this potato salad is wonderful, not to mention the soup. You went all out."

"Not really. I was making the soup when Emma called, and I decided to make the salad."

"You're a great cook," said Molly.

Stewart ducked his head, and his cheeks turned pinker. "Actually, cooking's my hobby."

"So did the Office Mart manager tell you anything?" Emma asked. She scooped up some potato salad on her fork.

"He said that he'd had to look at all the sales for the previous week and he didn't see where four empty boxes had been sold at the same time, just a few here and there. He said that the police were putting in a request for credit card records of the people who bought the boxes."

Molly told Stewart about what she'd found out from the downtown store and their conversation with Carmen. "We don't know if Carmen's the culprit, so we need to get as much info as possible."

After the dishes had been cleared off the table, Stewart asked to see the books that Jasper had carried from Emma's booth.

"Oh, *Mulberry Street*! I never read that one. A first?"

Emma beamed. "Yep. You may know this already, but one of the points is the boy's white shorts. In subsequent printings, the shorts are blue."

"I didn't know that. Remind me what a point is."

"It's something that signifies a first edition, like in some first edition books there is a misspelling that is corrected in later printings."

Stewart flipped through *A Child's Garden of Verses*. "Oh, I love Jessie Willcox Smith! I have some of her prints from *The Water Babies* and *The Princess and the Goblin*. I spent hours as a child reading. When I first saw her illustrations, my life opened up. I felt alive!"

Molly had been perusing Stewart's bookshelves. "Do you still have your childhood copy, or did you cut it up?"

"Molly," Stewart's voice sounded horrified. "I would *never*!"

"I was only kidding," Molly hastened to say.

Stewart walked to one of the bookshelves and handed Molly *A Child's Book of Stories*. He pointed to writing on the front free endpaper. "See—'Christmas 1988 from Aunt Eileen to Susan.' Aunt Eileen always gave us books for Christmas. She later said she didn't know what to buy for kids other than books."

"How great that must have been, always receiving books." Molly looked up. "And having an aunt and uncle who were booksellers." She flipped through *The Big Book of Fairy Tales*, stopping at a picture of Thumbelina on a lily pad surrounded by gaping fish.

Stewart said, "I loved Thumbelina. I wished I had a friend that I could carry around in my pocket. And the Frog Prince. He was changed from one form to another. Of course, growing up, I didn't know about Trans. People said if you could kiss your elbow, you could become a boy. I about lengthened my neck like Alice trying."

Emma pulled out *Alice in Wonderland*. "You have great stuff, Stewart."

"They're not firsts or anything. But well-loved. In fairy tales, or Wonderland, or Oz, anything is possible."

Chapter 21
Old Cars

L.M. (Lucy Maud) Montgomery, Anne of Green Gables, Boston: L.C. Page and Co., 1908. First edition. Illustrated by M.A. and W.A.J. Claus. Eight sepia toned illustrations. Tan ribbed cloth, gilt lettering on cover and spine. Illustrated pastedown on front board. Pictorial dust jacket.

Molly drove back across the Sunshine Parkway Bridge by herself because Emma and Stewart planned to go together to deliver the four books to Eileen. Then Stewart would bring Emma back to St. Pete where they would all have dinner at the Flying Dutchman tavern.

But now Molly was on her way to Manny and Son's Body Shop. The empty seat felt like Emma was still in it. Molly thought about Emma's reaction to her driving. She told herself not to take it personally. But she still felt it meant that Emma thought she was a careless driver. Molly felt confident about her driving.

Back on the island, Molly followed the navigation instructions of the "Bossy Lady" (her name for the voice in her phone) to Manny's. His shop was located in one of the old parts of St. Pete. She passed pebble-filled yards in front of small stucco houses. The body shop was on a corner facing a semi-busy street at right angles with a residential street.

Molly parked her van and threaded through the car lot, stopping to admire a restored Plymouth dating from the early fifties. Black, it gleamed in the afternoon sun. A chrome hood ornament of a ship topped the hood. "Cranbrook" was written on the side. The Plymouth must be Manny and Son's pet project.

A tall man with dark hair and bushy eyebrows came out of the office. He had on grease-stained blue jeans and a tight Tampa Bay Rays T-shirt. A tattoo of a monkey was on his left arm, and grease stains lay embedded in the folds of his hands and under his fingernails. Molly recognized him as Carmen's brother.

"Manny?"

"Yeah?" He squinted at her. "I'm the younger Manny."

"Molly. I met you through Carmen several years ago."

"If you say so." Younger Manny's eyes showed no glimmer of recognition.

"Somebody scraped against my van in a parking lot. My insurance company wants an estimate of the work."

"Let's take a look."

Molly hoped he couldn't tell that the scratch was six months old and that she had sideswiped her neighbor's car with her van, not the other way around. She wondered how she was going to query this brother who didn't remember her. Why should he? They had met only once, and Carmen had no doubt introduced many women to him.

When they reached her van, he walked around it and grinned. "Georgia? Hey, I remember you! You still have the 'I brake for hobbits' bumper sticker. I re-read *The Hobbit* and *Lord of the Rings* every couple of years. What's your name again?"

"Molly."

"Yeah, Carmen was into you. She said you were gonna come back and was torn up when you didn't."

"Oh—"

He waved. "Forget it. You don't have to apologize to me. I'm sure you had a good reason." He looked at the white line down the right side of the dark red van. "When did this happen?"

"Oh, um, a while ago. Couple of days."

"It's so easy to fix, if I was you, I wouldn't make a claim. I can fix it up with a little paint. I'll have to order it to match. Give me a day." He turned to her. "How long you gonna be in town?"

"I'm staying for a few days. I could bring it back later when my friend can drop me off."

"You stayin' with Carmen?"

She wanted to say, "Hell no!" but since he *was* Carmen's brother, she settled for, "I'm staying in a hotel downtown."

Manny said, "I don't blame you. I haven't spoken to her in two years myself. She's gotten herself into… Just be glad you got away from her when you did."

"What do you mean?" *Surely he knew Carmen was selling weed and cocaine back then. Was she selling worse, like heroin? Or was she into importing? That would be more dangerous.*

"Oh, you know Carmen. She's a mess." He waved his hand dismissively.

"Thanks, Manny. I'll bring the van early tomorrow morning."

Behind the wheel, Molly thought, *Manny hadn't spoken to Carmen in two years. That meant she had lied about the boxes. Why? Did she cut the pictures out? What was her reason?*

Chapter 22
Visiting Eileen

Washington Irving, The Legend of Sleepy Hollow, *London: George Harrap & Co., 1928. Green cloth with gilt lettering and illustration on front. Gilt lettering on spine, top edge gilt. Illustrated by Arthur Rackham. Eight color plates plus numerous black and white illustrations.*

As Emma rode with Stewart to Eileen's daughter's house in Clearwater, he filled her in about the relationships. "Melissa was adopted by Aunt Eileen and Uncle Jasper when they were in their forties. You know, back in the nineties when a lot of people were adopting girls from China."

They pulled up to one of the ubiquitous Florida stucco houses with ropy vines clambering around palm and rubber plants in the small front yard. Some clay pots lay on their sides, some broken, next to the door. Stewart knocked as Emma gave a heave to the book-laden cloth tote bag over her shoulder. Instantly the door flew open.

"Stewart!" Melissa wrapped her arms around Stewart and turned to Emma. "I'm sorry, I don't remember your name." An uncertain smile crossed her face, and she pushed a strand of black hair away from her forehead.

Emma stepped forward. "Hi, I'm Emma Clarke. We met a few days ago." *When your dad was murdered.* "I'm here to bring Eileen the books she bought from me."

Melissa nodded and led them down a hall to a long, light-filled room at the back of the house with jalousie windows, tiled floor, prints of ocean scenes on the walls, and tall potted plants—what inhabitants of the Sunshine State call a Florida room. A TV took up most of one wall. A peach-colored love seat sat at a right angle to a recliner where Eileen sat watching TV, a calico cat on her lap, and her foot, encased in its boot, on an ottoman. She wore her trademark silver barrettes, but one had slipped, hanging sidewise. She wore a long, faded, blue-and-burgundy print skirt and a white T-shirt. A paisley shawl in shades of burgundy, green, and gold was wrapped around her shoulders and arms. She looked up and gave them a weak smile. Stewart went over and kissed her on the cheek.

"Pretty cat," Emma said. "What's her name?" She knew that most calicos were female.

"Dinah," Melissa said. "You know, Alice in Wonderland's cat."

Emma held out her hand to the cat, who ignored it. "We brought you the books," she said, placing the tote bag by Eileen's ottoman. She turned to Melissa. "One of them is the Ralph Steadman *Alice.*"

"Cool. I collect *Alice* books."

"Oh, my," Emma said. "Maybe I shouldn't have said anything. Your dad might've bought it for you."

"Maybe, but I already have that one."

"I wasn't expecting you so soon," Eileen said. "Have a seat." She picked up the remote and turned the TV off.

Emma sat on the sofa, while Stewart took a wicker rocking chair. "We don't mean to bother you," Emma said.

"Oh, no, you're not bothering me. I'm glad to get the books. I want to look at them and price them as soon as I can. It'll take my mind off—well, you know. I got back online yesterday. Some of my books sold last Friday. I've got to get them off our database before someone else tries to buy them. Over the last year, we had to tell several people that the books they wanted had already been sold. Jasper was bad about keeping our listings up to date." She sighed.

Emma nodded her understanding. "I need to take a few off of BookHound myself."

"What's a book hound?" Stewart asked. "Sounds like a bookseller's dog."

Emma smiled as she thought of Molly's two Russian wolfhounds. *They* were certainly book hounds. "It's a database where booksellers catalog their books and upload the list to several bookselling sites."

"Would you all like something—iced tea, soda?" Melissa asked.

"I'm good," Stewart said.

"No, thanks," Emma replied.

Melissa said, "Okay. Mom, I'll be in the crafts room if you need anything." Dinah jumped down and followed her.

"Want to look at the books?" Emma asked.

"Yes, indeed. You told me about them, but it's not like seeing for myself."

As Emma pulled books out of the bag and put them one by one on Eileen's lap, Eileen seemed more animated with each new volume.

She held *Mulberry Street* and sniffed it. "Never held one of the true firsts before. Such good shape, too." Then she flipped through *Alice in Wonderland*. "I love Steadman's illustrations. So deliciously dark."

"Eileen," Emma said, plucking up her nerve, "Those books at the fair, the ones that someone stole and cut out the illustrations and returned the next day?" She paused. Eileen sat motionless. Emma went on, "You know a lot of booksellers. I was just wondering whether you have any ideas about who might have done it."

Eileen seemed to withdraw, shrinking into her shawl. Even her boot seemed to try to become smaller. "I have no idea," she said in a flat voice. "We had just got set up in the Coliseum. I hadn't been around, hadn't talked to any booksellers. Then, after what happened—" she hesitated. "Melissa and her husband Jim took down the booth Saturday morning. I didn't go back."

Emma said, "You've been around Clearwater, though, for a while. Do you happen to know about—well, any conflicts among booksellers?"

Eileen shook her head. "No, I don't."

"You've been here for, how long now?"

"I'm originally from Clearwater. We bought a house here about two years ago to be near Melissa and Jim and our granddaughter. And Stewart, of course. We've been going back and forth from Ohio to here. Now I'm here to stay."

Emma said, "One of the dealers said someone was trying to threaten them by mutilating their books." Eileen flinched.

Stewart spoke up. "I was confronted by some angry dealers on Sunday. I started going around to other print dealers to see if I could get any information. But no luck." Stewart jerked his thumb at Emma. "We three, including Molly, are going to try to figure out who did it. And we have a couple of leads."

Eileen looked alarmed. "You do?"

"Not much yet," Stewart said.

Eileen was quiet for a moment. "Why are you so interested in this?"

Emma said, "It was a horrible crime, damaging valuable books."

Eileen looked directly at her. "I suggest you drop it and

go home. Where are you from? Not here, right?"

"Atlanta." Emma got up her courage. "Eileen—do you know someone named Carmen?"

"Carmen who?" Eileen's eyes narrowed.

What is her last name? Emma thought. She remembered seeing it on the mailbox. "Esposito."

Eileen's head jerked up.

She knows her! Emma thought. Her heart jumped into her throat.

Eileen said in an even voice, "Stewart, would you get my purse over there and pull out my checkbook, please?" She looked at the receipt that Emma had included, wrote a check, and handed it to Emma. "Listen, I'm getting tired. If you don't mind, I'd like to go lie down. Thanks for bringing the books."

"Are you sure you don't know Carmen Esposito?" Emma felt her heart pound even more.

Eileen drew herself into the shawl more tightly. She said in a low voice, "Are you working with the police? Or…?" She left the word hanging.

"No one except Stewart and Molly. We're just asking questions."

"Then, like I said, give this up and go home. You don't know what you're getting into. And you leave it alone, too, Stewart."

Stewart leaned toward her. "What do you know, Aunt Eileen?"

Eileen shook her head and looked away.

Stewart said softly, "Please tell us."

"Honey, listen to me. I think I know who killed Jasper."

"Who?" Emma whispered.

Eileen looked at her, eyes wide. "I got a threatening phone call. Don't ask me anymore. Just—be careful. Go back to Atlanta and forget about all this."

"But…"

"I mean it. Since the call, I don't go out, not anywhere. Melissa asked the police to keep a watch on the house. They said they would. This is bigger than you *and* the print business *and* the book business. Stewart says you've been going around asking questions. I'm warning you, stop right now. You might just end up asking questions of the wrong person."

Emma asked, still in a whisper, "What do you think it's about?"

Eileen said nothing.

"Okay." Emma looked at Stewart. "We're going now, Eileen. Take care."

"Tell Melissa to come help me. I'd like to go lie down." She looked again at Emma and gave a tiny smile. "Thanks for bringing the books."

"Eileen, if you think of anything…"

"Take care of yourselves. Be safe." She reached for Stewart's hand and gripped it tight. "Oh, Honey, I'm so sorry about all this. I never thought we'd get you involved."

Chapter 23
Comparing Notes

Felix Salten (Siegmund Saltzmann), Bambi, A Life in the Woods, *New York: Simon and Schuster, 1928. First American edition. Originally published in German in 1923. Translated from the German by Whittaker Chambers. Illustrated by Kurt Wiese. Original green vertical-ribbed cloth, gilt lettering on spine, gilt rule on head and tail. Front cover with deer motif in gilt. Pictorial endpapers. Frontispiece and 25 color plates, black and white illustrations throughout. Title page printed in black and green.*

Molly, Emma, and Stewart sat on the porch of The Flying Dutchman that overlooked a row of flowering hibiscus bushes. Ceiling fans whirred gently, lifting the corners of the white tablecloth on their glass-top table. A double row of tables with rattan chairs, most of them empty, lined the long, rectangular porch. Their table was on the outer edge, and Molly rested her elbow on the iron railing.

Molly had just described her visit to the body shop. She finished by saying, "Manny hasn't even *talked* to Carmen for years."

"So, she obviously didn't need boxes to help her brother

move." Emma took a sip of her pinot grigio.

"How well do you know this Carmen?" Stewart asked.

Molly looked at Emma. "Not well, actually. We had a brief fling about five years ago." She felt her cheeks flushing. "I found out she wasn't exactly ethical."

Emma said, "When we asked Eileen if she knew Carmen, it was clear that she did. And that warning she gave us—" She shook her head. "She's scared."

"So, Carmen lied, Eileen is afraid to even tell us who called her, and you two are told to return to Atlanta." Stewart sipped his beer.

"Right," said Molly. "And Eileen thinks she knows who killed Jasper."

"*And*," Emma added, "Most important—she thinks Jasper's killing and the books being defaced are related."

"Did she say that?" Molly asked.

"She implied that it's all linked. She said, 'This is bigger than you and the book business and the print business.'"

Stewart nodded. "That's what I thought."

At that moment, Stewart's phone let out the opening strains of "Ain't Misbehaving." He peered at the screen. "It's Melissa. I better take this." He stood up and walked over to the other side of the porch where no one was sitting.

Emma said, "Molly, tomorrow is Thursday. Why don't we call the detectives in the morning so we can tell them about what we've discovered so far. We can ask if they need us to stay 'til Friday. If they don't, we could head home."

Molly looked at her steadily. "Do you want to?"

"Maybe." Emma took a swallow of her wine.

Molly felt a lump of disappointment.

The waiter arrived. As they had asked, he had split the salmon over the mushroom and spinach risotto in two dishes. He placed a dish in front of Molly and one in front of Emma. He placed a dish of angel hair pasta topped with pesto at Stewart's place.

"Guys," Stewart said, returning to the table. "That was Melissa. She waited until Eileen went to sleep to call." He took a deep breath. "She thinks drugs are involved."

Molly looked at Stewart with narrowed eyes. "How?"

"Melissa thinks Uncle Jasper got involved in the drug trade."

"Eileen said they were like hippies before there *were* hippies," Emma said. "I'm not surprised they might have smoked some weed—"

Stewart interrupted, "This is more than a little weed. Melissa says she remembers, on their way home from St. Pete, they always went to Columbus, and her dad would pull up to a warehouse and talk to some guys while she and her mom would walk up the street and get ice cream."

Emma said, "That does sound like they might have been delivering drugs. But what does it have to do with Jasper being murdered?"

Stewart continued, "Melissa tried to talk to her mother about it, and Eileen told Melissa that the less she knew the better."

The waiter appeared again and set down Stewart's second pint.

"Bon appétit." Stewart took a swallow and swirled angel hair pasta onto his fork.

The three friends ate silently for a few moments.

Molly turned to Stewart. "What do you think about Eileen's warning?"

"She might be right. We *don't* know what we're getting into."

Molly said, "Stewart, did you have any idea about what Jasper and Eileen were up to? Didn't anything ever look suspicious?"

Stewart shrugged. "I know it sounds funny, but I didn't. When I got into the print selling business, I didn't go to the same places they did. I sold at flea markets, and then got a booth in a consignment mall. They were middle-to-high-end booksellers, going to New York, Boston, San Francisco. Our paths didn't cross except in the past few years when I started selling at St. Pete. I'd tell them about what I was doing, but I wasn't part of their world."

Molly nodded. "That makes sense." She watched a group of gray-haired men and women doing Tai Chi on the lawn beside the rec center across the street. She felt a moment's envy. *They* weren't trying to figure out who killed someone and mutilated some books. She took a bite of salmon and asked, "So what's next?"

Emma put down her fork. "I can't get Eileen's warning out of my mind."

"I wonder if she does know who killed Jasper?"

"And if she does, why won't she go to the police?" Stewart asked.

A tall man in overalls, a railroad cap, and a long white beard approached the table. "Stewart! Hey, man." His face lit up with a warm, humorous smile.

"Ty!" Stewart exclaimed, springing to his feet. "What's up?" The two men grasped hands and gave each other a half-hug. Stewart sat down again and said, "These are my friends, Molly and Emma. They're booksellers."

Ty touched his railroad cap. "Pleased to meet you." He turned toward Stewart. "How was your show?"

"Not bad. Except I guess you heard about Jasper."

Ty grimaced. "Oh man, that was awful. I've known Jasper Ross for ages. So hard to think of him dead. You know what?" He took a deep breath. "I think I may have been the last person to see Jasper alive. Other than the one that killed him."

"What?" Stewart said. "Where did you see him?"

"I met him in the bar here Friday afternoon to buy some books. I've already been to the police and told them all about it."

"Ty, did you know anything about—" Stewart started, but stopped. "Never mind."

Ty looked at the young man, brow furrowed in a question. When Stewart didn't say anything else, he said to Molly and Emma, "Well, it was nice to meet you. I better take off." He raised his cap and strode away.

"I'll be back in a minute." Stewart got up and went inside. Molly was glad that the restroom was labeled "All Genders."

After Stewart was out of sight, Molly said, "Emma, since the police told us to stay until Friday, do you still want to leave Saturday morning?"

"I don't know. How about you?"

Molly felt torn. She felt a yearning desire for the quiet haven of her home and sweet dog kisses. But she also wanted to find out what happened to Jasper and who mutilated the books. And she was enjoying her time with Emma.

Molly took a sip of beer. "Emma," she said, "I'm going to admit it—I don't want to let this go. And I especially want us to find *East of the Sun*. I feel partly responsible for your buying such an expensive book. It's important to me that we find it."

Emma said, "Thank you. That's really important to me."

A cool breeze raised goose bumps on Molly's arm. "As much as I hate to, I think we should follow up with Carmen. I mean, she *did* lie about her brother. So maybe she lied about other things."

"Right." Emma popped a forkful of salmon into her mouth.

Molly looked at her intently. "And because I want us to. It's more fun with you."

Emma put her fork down. "Oh, it's fun to go see Carmen, is it?"

"Carmen needs to answer some questions! We're not going to let her off the hook so easily again."

"Good luck with that," Emma said. "Remember how she kept changing the subject every time you tried to ask her anything?"

"Let's talk about it more tonight."

"Okay." Emma took the last sip of her wine.

Stewart returned. "I think I better get home. It's been great hanging out with you guys, even under the circumstances. Give me a call and let me know what you decide. If you want to pursue finding out who stole the books, I'm game. And if not, well, I might just do it on my own."

"Emma and I will talk more tonight about what we're going to do," Molly said.

"Okay. Let me know what you decide," Stewart said. "As for me, I'm going to see Aunt Eileen again." He stood up. "And find out what she's *not* telling her daughter."

೧೨೦೩

Molly and Emma walked side by side along the pier in the growing dusk. The sun was sinking below the line of dark water in the bay. Streaks of pink, peach, and glowing liquid gold swirled across the darkening sky. Molly's sandals made a soft plopping sound against the weathered wood of the pier. She cast glances at Emma, who almost glided in her black leather sandals. Her nearly sheer lavender tunic seemed to float around her hips over capri leggings. Silver highlights lit up her dark hair in the dusk. Molly thought, *what was it about Emma?*

"You're quiet," Emma said in a soft voice.

"Just thinking."

"Thinking about what?"

"Ah—about tomorrow. What we're going to do."

"Are you sure you're not looking forward to seeing

Carmen again?"

"Oh, Emma," Molly said with a sigh. "Please don't think I hold any more feelings about her at all."

"Does it matter what I think?" Emma said, almost inaudibly.

"Yes, it does! It matters a lot." Molly stopped walking.

Emma stood still. A pelican, perched on a post, was looking out over the bay. "You don't have to explain anything to me." Emma said softly.

"Emma, I'm not trying…to…" Molly felt as though her words were swelling up through her throat, each one about to stick. "I mean, I don't want you to think, not just that Carmen is nothing, but that *you* are *something* to me, uh, that is…"

Emma turned to her, an inquisitive eyebrow arched.

Molly said, still choking on her words. "You're an important person to me, Emma. I value you…what you think." Her words felt inadequate.

"Listen, Molly, we were getting close last year but after I was gone so long, when I got back, I felt a little awkward. But after the last few days, I'm feeling closer to you than ever."

Molly stood very still. "I feel it, too. That we both care for each other. Isn't that what matters?"

Emma nodded. They stood close enough for Molly to feel Emma's breath. Emma leaned in and gave her friend a quick kiss on the lips and backed away.

It was a kiss that didn't invite another, but didn't prohibit it, either. Molly felt as though fireworks had just gone off in her chest.

Chapter 24
Detail Work

Hans Christian Andersen, Fairy Tales, *Philadelphia: David McKay, 1932. Brick red cloth, gilt lettering on spine and front, decorative endpapers. Illustrated by Arthur Rackham. Twelve color plates, black and white illustrations throughout.*

Emma and Molly stayed up late discussing how to get the truth out of Carmen, and they decided it was best for Molly to go by herself. Then Emma took a bath, using her nice bath salts. When she got back to the bedroom, Molly was fast asleep snoring. Emma, disappointed, slipped between the sheets of her own bed.

First thing in the morning, Emma suggested that Molly call Carmen. "You don't want to show up unexpectedly," she said. She didn't add *and interrupt a drug deal.*

"Good idea." Molly sat on the edge of her bed, punching in the number, her short, wavy hair falling in a lock over her forehead. Emma wanted to push it back.

"Hi, Carmen? This is Molly."

Emma heard Carmen's voice over the line: "What do you want, Molly?"

Molly said, "I just thought of a few things I'd like to talk to you about." A few indecipherable words from Carmen, and Molly said, "After four, then. See ya." She turned her phone off. "You're right. She says she'll be busy until after four."

"So now to Manny's. I'll follow you."

After dropping off Molly's van at Manny's, Emma drove them back to downtown St. Pete. They ate breakfast at the café near the police station. "While we're here," Emma said, "Let's call the detectives and see if they need to see us today."

Molly chewed her buckwheat pancake. After swallowing, she asked, "You wanna call 'em?"

"Sure." Emma spread strawberry jam on her biscuit. "After breakfast."

Today's waitress had gray hair and a friendly face, and she was quick to come around with the coffee pot. She scurried from one table to another, refilling cups, bringing orders, and giving each of the customers a smile and a few friendly words.

A small park across from the café was half in shade. Emma and Molly sat on an iron bench in a gazebo while Emma called Detective Rodriguez. Molly watched three little children playing on a geodesic dome while two women sat nearby talking and laughing.

"He asked us to come in at two this afternoon," Emma said. "More information has come to light, and he said he was going to reach out to us today anyway."

"I wonder what it's about."

"Where are we going today before the police?"

"There are a couple of antique malls in Tampa that Stewart said he wasn't familiar with."

"Tampa sounds good. I've never been there."

ᖇᖇᖇ

After going through two antique malls looking fruitlessly for anyone who sold prints, Emma and Molly enjoyed Cuban sandwiches at a bodega in Ybor City. Emma ordered a Mexican Coke. At Molly's inquiring glance, she said, "They're made with real sugar, not corn syrup. And they taste better."

After lunch, the two headed back to the police station. This time they didn't have to wait but were immediately ushered into Rodriguez's office. When they walked in, they saw Rodriguez behind his desk and a stocky, brown-skinned man in a suit with close-cropped, graying hair standing next to Rodriguez's desk.

"Hi, ladies," Rodriguez said. "This is Detective Bedford. He's working with us on this case."

Bedford leaned forward and shook their hands in turn as they introduced themselves.

Rodriguez said, "Have a seat." He indicated the three straight chairs in front of his desk.

Detective Bedford moved a chair so that he was looking directly at the two women. He fixed his eyes on Molly and then Emma. "Do you two happen to know two guys named Ari and Nick Alexander?"

Emma asked, "From Ari's?"

He nodded.

"During the book fair, I met Nick when we ordered lunch from Ari's. When we went to Tarpon Springs on Monday, we ate lunch at Mt. Olympus, and he was there. Then we saw on a brochure that the two places are connected."

"What was he doing when you saw him at the book fair?"

"He came to my booth with another dealer."

"Who was the dealer?"

"Mignon Chambray."

"Where did they go after leaving your booth?"

"Mignon headed toward her booth, and Nick turned at the end of my aisle. He was carrying large bags, and I assumed he was taking lunches to people."

"Did Ms. Chambray remain in her booth for the next thirty to sixty minutes?"

Emma said, "I'm not sure. I don't think she was there the whole time."

Molly said, "When I was carrying my lunch back, I saw her walking around talking on her phone."

"Walking around where?" Bedford asked.

"I saw her walking in front of Over the Hills and Far Away."

"Did you see Nick walking around at that time?"

"I didn't know who Nick was, and I didn't really notice anybody carrying bags. I was only thinking about getting back to my booth so I could eat my lunch."

"Over the Hills and Far Away? That was one of the booths that had books stolen, right?"

"That's right."

"Who are the other booksellers whose books were damaged?"

"Jeff Wilkes, Bob Helm, Lynda Duvall, Chris Kraken, and—can you think of anyone else, Molly?"

Molly shook her head.

"Not everyone was affected?" Bedford asked.

"No," Emma answered. "That's one of the odd things about this."

"So, it was only about five booksellers whose books were damaged, out of about how many—two hundred?"

"A hundred and fifty total," Molly said.

"Do these five have anything in common, do you know?"

Molly thought for a moment and shook her head.

Rodriguez asked, "Do you know any connection between these five book dealers and Jasper Ross?"

"The only connection I can think of is Jerry because he also sells children's books. The others all have different specialties."

"What about the other booksellers? Any of them have a grudge against Jasper Ross or his wife?"

Molly shook her head. "Not that I know of."

Emma said, "Me neither."

"Anything else we need to know?"

Emma hesitated. She hated getting Stewart involved, but she didn't want to withhold information. "I visited Eileen. She got a threatening phone call. I don't know from whom. She told me to stop asking questions and go home. And her nephew said that drugs might be involved."

The two detectives looked at each other. They both scribbled something on legal pads.

Rodriguez shoved back his chair. "Are you both planning on going back to Atlanta soon?"

"We'll probably go back tomorrow," Emma said.

Bedford got to his feet. "Thanks for your help."

Rodriguez stood. "And we have your phone numbers, so we may call you if we need information."

Molly and Emma both stood up and shook hands with Rodriguez and Bedford.

Outside, Molly said, "Let's go get my van."

⊱⊰

As Emma pulled onto the street, she said, "That was unexpected. What did you think of that guy Bedford?"

Molly said, "Yeah. He didn't ask us any questions related to the murder. He must be investigating the book thefts."

"It sounds like they're making a connection now between the books and the murder."

"And all those questions about Nick and Mignon? It

sounds as though the police think *they're* involved in the thefts."

Emma turned a corner. "Mignon isn't my favorite person, but I just can't believe she would steal books from other dealers."

"Let alone cut them up."

"And why would Nick and Ari be involved in cutting up books?"

Emma shook her head and pulled into Manny's lot. "See you back at the hotel."

The van stood parked in front, looking shiny. The white streak was gone, and the whole vehicle looked as though it had been through a car wash.

While Manny was writing up her bill, Molly looked around his shop. It looked and smelled like every car repair shop she had ever been in: organized clutter, magazines, all kinds of car-related junk; the odors of gasoline and oil permeated the air. A glass case stood behind the metal desk with an electric fan ensconced on top, its green paint flaking off. The case contained models of iconic autos like the Corvette, the Mustang, and Molly's favorite, the Thunderbird. A pile of used spark plugs completed the still life under glass.

"You do really good detail work, Manny," Molly said. "I can't even tell where that white scrape was." She got out her debit card.

"Thanks," Manny said. "Here's your keys."

After she paid, she said, "Thanks for doing such a good job and so quickly. I really appreciate it."

Molly turned to leave the shop. "By the way," she said in a voice she hoped sounded offhand, "Carmen said she was helping you move last weekend."

"She's full of it," Manny said with a snort. "Like I said, I haven't seen her in three years."

I thought last time, he said he hadn't talked to her in two years, Molly thought. "She said that was why she got a bunch of boxes from the office supply store. Big boxes."

Manny shrugged.

Molly didn't like to push, but she felt she had to. "Do you have any idea what she might have wanted them for?"

Manny was starting to look uncomfortable. "Nah. Carmen's business is her own." He leaned over the counter. "And you could get in a lotta trouble, lady, if you go on asking questions. Like I said, I don't want to get involved in any of Carmen's doings. Ever since she got mixed up with those Greek brothers—" He stopped and looked at one of the work orders on the counter. Several clipboards with keys attached were scattered on the glass top.

Molly's pulse began to pound. "What Greek brothers? Not the guys that run Ari's?"

A mulberry flush spread over Manny's forehead and jaws. "Look, I didn't say anything. I gotta get back to work." He picked up one of the clipboards and turned away.

Molly went to her van, glancing in the back out of habit. The books in their wooden crates looked untouched. She pulled out of the lot. As she passed the cinderblock building, she saw Manny standing half in shadow in the doorway, watching her drive away.

Chapter 25
Deliveries

Carolyn Keene, The Secret of the Old Clock, Nancy Drew Mystery Series, *New York: Grosset and Dunlap, 1930. Blue boards with orange lettering on front cover, black lettering on spine. Frontispiece and three other illustrations by Russell Tandy.*

Emma pulled into the crushed seashell parking lot. Once more, the only parking space was in front of the dumpster, surrounded by fast food cartons and glass bottles. She remembered the tan jacket sleeve sticking out from behind that dumpster. Had it really been only one week earlier? The book fair seemed only a couple of days ago, but it also felt like months. Years.

A small silver hatchback with a red magnetic sign on the door that read "Ari's—Simply the BEST Falafel!" pulled up by the back door. Nick got out, opened the back door, and loaded himself down with bags and boxes. He went in through the hotel's rear entrance.

They must do a great delivery business, thought Emma. He'd been friendly when she'd met him. Maybe he was Mignon's boyfriend. But she was with the bald guy Friday night at dinner.

Emma had just gotten to the room when Molly called. "Do I have something to tell you!"

"What? Did you find out something?"

"The Greek brothers!" Molly said in a lowered voice. "Manny said Carmen was mixed up with the Greek brothers."

"Ari's?"

"Don't know. There are a lot of Greeks in the Tarpon Springs area. But Manny realized he'd said too much and warned me to stop asking questions."

"But that's the second person who has warned us." Then Emma thought of something. "Wait a minute! I just realized that the books were stolen at lunch time, right? That's when Ari's brought the meals. They knew who ordered food and would be out of their booths picking up their orders."

"Damn! I'll bet that's right." Molly thought a moment. "Hey, maybe Mignon was on her phone to Nick, telling him what booths to go to!"

Emma put in, "And what books to take!"

"And all the while being a lookout! Because when I passed her, she was just pacing back and forth—in front of Jerry's booth."

"That *was* fishy, Nick carrying those bags since Kitty announced for the dealers to go to the back to pick our lunches." Emma said. "And why didn't I think it looked odd, him carrying those bags? Then they carried the books in the delivery boxes out of the Coliseum. They cut out the pictures, put the books in boxes that Carmen bought and brought them back and left them on the porch."

"What have they done with the illustrations?" Molly asked. "I'll have to ask Carmen."

"Be careful, Mol. I'm serious."

"I will. I don't think I'll be there long. When we get back, we can decide where to go for supper. See you soon,

Sherlock."

Emma heard Molly's engine start up. She settled into the hotel room and stretched out on the thick comforter. She glanced around. It was the first time she had really looked at the old-fashioned room. The walls were a faint yellow, and a large screen television hung on the wall between two paintings of Tampa Bay, one with lights on tall buildings across the bay and reflected moonlight on the water's surface. The other one had a clear blue sky with sail boats dotted on the water. It was the same view from the St. Pete Pier. Her thoughts kept returning to last Friday—finding Jasper's body, his skin that same grey pallor as her dad's—and to Saturday—the thefts. Her mind kept going round and round. *What is the connection between Nick and Ari and Carmen? Are they involved in the drug trade? And what does stealing books have to do with drugs?* Then she remembered Jerry saying, "They did it to threaten us."

She got up, sat at the desk, and began writing down notes on her writing pad.

She jumped when she heard her phone ring. It was Stewart. "Hey, Emma. I couldn't get ahold of Molly."

"She's driving. She's funny about answering the phone while driving."

Stuart chuckled. "So old fashioned."

"If you've ever ridden with Molly, you'd not want her to talk while driving. I mean, she tends to drive faster than I'm comfortable with."

"Are you with her now?"

"No. She went by herself to Carmen's."

She heard a loud sigh. "Some shit went down today. I need to talk to you guys."

"What happened?"

"I went over to Melissa's to see Aunt Eileen. I wanted to ask her more about who she thought killed Uncle Jasper or who she thought called to threaten her. But she wouldn't open up.

"Then Melissa said, 'Mom, maybe it's time to tell what you and Dad were really doing when you stopped in Columbus every year after the book fair.' Aunt Eileen said, 'You knew?' Melissa said, 'I've suspected for years. You and I would always go get ice cream while Dad talked to some guys at that warehouse.' Then it all tumbled out."

Emma said, "What tumbled out?"

"Turns out she and Jasper had been moving cocaine from Florida to Ohio for years. They were regular drug mules. Every spring after the book fair they hid coke in amongst the books. Eileen didn't want to do it, but Jasper kept telling her they could no longer support themselves just by selling books. When they told their Florida contact they were retiring and wouldn't be able to continue, they said, 'You could just take a trip once a year to see your friends in Ohio, couldn't you?' But Jasper insisted that they wouldn't anymore. After cajoling and threatening, the person said, 'You'll live to regret this.'"

"Did she know who it was?"

"She wouldn't tell me. She absolutely refused. Maybe it was the same person who just called her."

"Oh, god," Emma said.

"Well, now we have a motive."

"But why kill him?"

"Maybe they first wanted to scare him. Then it escalated."

"Why at the hotel? An arranged meeting? One that Eileen wouldn't know about?"

"Could be. She won't say any more. I think she regrets telling me so much already. She was really shaken. Melissa will call me tonight after her mother goes to bed."

"Whew." Emma exhaled. "Thanks for letting me know, Stewart. I'll tell Molly when she gets back." She suddenly thought of where Molly was.

"Oh no! Molly's at Carmen's now. She went back to ask some more questions. But if Carmen's involved with the same people as Eileen and Jasper were, Molly might be in danger. I think I'll call her and warn her."

⁊⊰⊱⁊

However, when Emma called Molly's number, she got her voice mail. *She must still be driving*, she thought. Emma turned off her phone and sank back onto the bed. *Oh, god, Molly,* she thought. *I hope you're okay. I should have gone with you.*

She started making notes in her spiral notebook. She listed the people who sounded suspicious. Molly suspected Carmen of knowing more about the books than she had said before, but what about Jasper's murder? Could Carmen be involved in that too? She kept seeing Eileen telling her to go home. And now Manny warning them also. If only she had dissuaded Molly from going to Carmen's.

Chapter 26
Carmen in the Carport

Wanda Gag, Millions of Cats, New York: Coward McCann, 1928. Illustrated by the author. First edition with Jersey City Printing Company on the copyright page. Oblong, illustrated yellow boards, illustrated throughout. Pictorial dust jacket. Won Newbery Honor award in 1929, one of the few picture books to do so. The oldest American picture book still in print.

As soon as Molly swung the van into Carmen's driveway, she saw Carmen standing in the open carport. Molly had called ahead to make sure she was at home, but she was surprised to see her waiting outside.

Carmen wore another caftan, this one with butterflies and hummingbirds on it. A metallic bird's blue throat shone in the afternoon sunlight. On her feet were long, pointy, embroidered mules, looking like something a denizen of a harem would wear.

When Molly got out of the van, Carmen glanced at the van. "Where's your friend?" Her voice sounded distinctly less warm than it had yesterday. "Why are you here, Molly?"

Startled, Molly felt off guard. After all, she was the one planning to ask questions. She said, hoping her voice sounded firm, "I came back to ask you a few more questions."

Carmen's brown eyes narrowed. "Oh, did you?" She glared at Molly. "Why are you going around asking questions?"

Molly took a step backward. Carmen's change in attitude had thrown her off. "I just wanted to ask you again about those banker's boxes. Why did you buy them?"

"Are you working for the police?"

"No!" Molly protested.

Carmen hovered over Molly.

Molly felt the impulse to step back again, but she didn't want to let Carmen bully her, so she stood her ground. "Look, Carmen, we're probably leaving tomorrow morning. But I want to find out from you why you lied about those boxes."

"Molly. Go home. Nothing good can come of you asking questions."

So, Carmen does know something.

"I know you're good at moving on," Carmen continued, her voice angrier. "Cutting off communication, acting like you don't know me—until you need something. So, let's just leave it at that. Go now." Carmen craned her neck around as a hatchback careened into the driveway behind Molly's van. The driver stepped out, brown-skinned, short dark hair. Molly's pulse started to race. Nick. He stalked toward Molly.

Before Molly could say anything, the young man pressed a gun to her temple and grasped her arm. Molly felt as though a bucket of ice had been dumped over her. She couldn't move or think.

Carmen said quietly, "I tried to warn you."

"You and your friend pushed too much," her assailant

hissed. "Going around asking people questions. Call your friend. I want to talk to her."

Molly wondered, *Who other than Carmen told about us asking questions? One of the print dealers?* She pulled her phone out of her back pocket.

"Now call her!" He bumped the handgun against her temple. She flinched. She could taste the Cuban sandwich she'd had for lunch. Hand shaking, she pressed Emma's name. Emma answered almost before it rang.

"Emma," Molly said, her voice croaking. "I'm at Carmen's with a gun to my head."

"Molly!"

"Emma, get out of town now…!" She shrieked as Nick hit her on the side of the head with the barrel of the gun. The pain was so bad that she couldn't think for a moment.

Nick shouted into her phone, "Listen, bitch. Pack up both of your stuff in your suitcases and get over here to Carmen's, or you won't be seeing your friend no more, get it?"

"What?!"

"If you're not here in half an hour, I'll call you again and you'll hear your friend's brains being blown out. Don't even think about calling the police, understand?"

A little voice said, "Yes. What's the address again?"

Nick cursed. "Fifty-nine thirty-two Fifty-ninth Avenue."

"Okay. I'll be there soon." Emma's voice almost faded out.

"You better." Nick punched the phone off and shoved Molly. "Now get on, we're going in the house."

Molly's head throbbed where he hit her. She barely registered that Nick had given Carmen her phone.

Chapter 27
Someone Unexpected

Mark Twain, The Adventures of Huckleberry Finn, *London: Chatto and Windus, 1884. First edition, precedes the U.S. publication. Red cloth with gilt lettering on spine. Front cover has gilt lettering and black silhouette figures.*

Emma pressed her phone to her chest, breathing hard. She closed her eyes and made herself take slow breaths. Her mind kept going over and over *whattodowhattodowhattodo?* She sat on the bed and looked around, as though to get advice from the bedspread or framed pictures. Would whoever had Molly be likely to let her go free and safe? No, her realistic side told her. On the other hand, if she did not go, Molly definitely would be killed. She couldn't just sit by and do nothing. Besides, she had a gun. She smiled grimly to herself.

She hastened to pack up Molly's belongings and her own, stuffing the two suitcases and numerous tote bags into every available space in her car and just managing to get it all packed. She raced to the desk to check out and tore out of the parking lot and headed towards Carmen's.

Emma wondered whether she should have turned right, not left, at that last light, to get to Carmen's house. None of the streets and houses looked familiar. Her surroundings looked even more like Old Florida than ever, with weeds growing wild everywhere, vines tangled around fences, and clumps of sea grapes by the street and in the yards. The subdivisions looked as though they had been built in the 1940s or earlier. She saw fewer houses, some built of crumbling stucco, and unpainted frame houses with falling-down front porches.

Then she saw "59th" and turned. But she realized that this was not Carmen's street. *Omygod,* she thought. *Did I take a wrong turn?* Looking to one side and then the other, she realized with a sickening lurch in her stomach that she had seen none of these houses before. Each block looked more decrepit than the last, and the vegetation in the yards looked thicker and more crushing. She decided she had better stop and pulled over onto the shoulder. A small vacant lot lay behind a dilapidated wire fence. She thought, *I'm lost. Who would know where I am?* The answer came to her immediately, Stewart. He might know where she was and how to get to Carmen's. Emma seized her phone and punched Stewart's number. *Please, please answer*, she begged silently. On the fourth ring, Stewart answered.

"Hey, what's up?"

Emma almost sobbed at the sound of the familiar voice. "Stewart, I need help. I'm lost, and I need to get to Molly. She's in danger."

"What?" Stewart's voice sharpened. "Danger? What are you talking about?"

Emma spilled out everything that had happened since Molly's call. She finished with, "And I know it's dangerous to go, but I have to get to Molly."

"You're right the first time," Stewart said in a hard voice. "You must *not* go into that situation alone. Who talked to you?"

"I didn't ask who it was. Someone at Carmen's."

"Must be what Eileen warned us about. Carmen's involved in drug trafficking, and Molly walked into the middle of it." Stewart was quiet for a second. Emma could hear him breathing. "Where did you say you were?"

Emma went to the map app on her phone. The tear-shaped red indicator showed that she was near the intersection of two streets she had never heard of. She told Stewart her location.

He said, "My friend Ty might be able to help. You remember him—y'all met him at the Dutchman last night?"

"The guy with the beard?"

"Yeah. He lives not far from there," Stewart said. "I'll give him a call. He used to be a police detective. Stay where you are, okay? If I can't get hold of Ty, I'll call you back."

"Okay but tell him to hurry!"

Emma opened the window and breathed the humid Florida air. Dry cicada song pulsated from the trees. She almost thought the sound was in her head, it rattled so loud. It was a sound that she had always found peaceful before. Now it sounded sinister, frightening. She looked around. A driveway nearby wound off into the shrubs and trees. Clumps of palm, yucca, white oak, and vines tangled around everything. A rusty metal mailbox teetered on a wooden post. She peered at a hand-lettered sign that read in almost obliterated letters, "NO SOLICITING."

An antique blue pickup truck pulled up and stopped on the shoulder in front of her. As she watched, the driver got out of the cab. She recognized the man from the restaurant.

"Hey," he said. "I'm Ty Olson. You're Stewart's friend, right?"

Emma answered, "Yes, I'm Emma. You got here fast."

"I just live over a block from here. Lucky Stewart got me while I was at home."

"Thanks so much for coming." She opened her glove compartment, slipped a small revolver into her handbag, and got out of the car.

Ty's unruly white beard flowed over the front of his overalls, and his grey-white hair curled from under his broad-brimmed straw hat. He must have been working with paints, as his hands were streaked with colors, and his faded overalls were festooned with what looked like paint streaks.

Emma asked, "Did Stewart tell you about Molly? What's happening?"

Ty nodded. "Where is she?"

"She's at Carmen Esposito's house on 59th Street. But this doesn't look familiar. I have to get there right away!"

"Are you sure you don't mean 59th Avenue?" Ty asked.

Emma suddenly realized that Carmen lived on 59th Avenue. "You're right."

"That's about ten miles from here. You must of got your streets and your avenues mixed up. People visiting St. Pete do that a lot."

Emma nodded. "Right. But I need to get to Molly!"

"I live right around the corner from here. Follow me and we'll leave your car there."

Emma hesitated. The books, her stuff! She couldn't stop thinking, *We'll be too late! Carmen's friends will kill Molly.*

After leaving her car in Ty's driveway, Emma climbed into his passenger seat. Emma glanced at him and could just see the outline of what looked like a shoulder holster under the left side of his overalls. "I have to tell you I have a gun in my purse. I thought maybe I could help."

Ty asked, "Can you use it?"

"I've been shooting since I was nine years old."

"I've got a gun too." He patted his chest over the shoulder holster.

She let out her breath.

The smell of old truck permeated her nostrils. She noted,

in spite of her anxiety, the chrome handle that pushed out the triangular window, a welcome necessity in vehicles in the days before air conditioning, the dashboard with its radio dial and buttons, the glove compartment, half spilling open with what looked like receipts of oil changes and other car work.

The lengthening shadows and deep gold of the sun stretched out over the road as Ty turned the key and the truck roared into life. They raced back the way Emma had come, bouncing over the uneven streets. Emma grabbed the loop that hung next to her head. *Convenient little thing,* she thought. *These old vehicles had some great features.*

"Tell me more about what's going on," Ty said.

Emma hesitated. "I don't know everything, but my friend Molly is in trouble. She called me and this guy told me to pack our stuff and get over there."

"You don't really believe they are going to let both of you go?"

Emma said, "Probably not, but I have to get to her."

Ty asked, "How are you and your friend mixed up with them, if I may ask?"

"We haven't done anything wrong," Emma said. "We're booksellers. We were trying to find out who killed Jasper Ross. And who mutilated some books from the book fair. We think they're connected. Molly thought this friend of hers, Carmen, might know something about it."

"What made her think that?"

"Cardboard boxes. The books were stolen and then returned in new banker's boxes with their illustrations cut out. Molly found out that someone driving a vintage car, like Carmen's, had bought some boxes like that on Saturday." As she spoke, she felt that it all sounded so speculative, so far-fetched.

But Ty didn't laugh. "Huh," he said. He didn't say anything more for a minute or two. Added, "We know about

Carmen."

"What—what do you know?" Emma asked. "Do you mean—the police?"

Ty nodded. "I was on the force, as Stewart may have told you. Retired twelve years ago, but I still help out when I'm needed. Carmen's been under surveillance a few times, but nothing stuck."

They sped on down the street, Emma holding on for dear life to the loop. She tried to suppress her growing panic.

Chapter 28
Do a Line!

Hugh Lofting, The Story of Doctor Dolittle, *New York: Frederick A. Stokes Company, 1923. First edition. The first book in the Doctor Dolittle series. Illustrated by the author. Orange cloth boards, color pictorial pastedown and blue lettering and embellishments. Pictorial endpapers. Full-page color frontispiece with black and white illustrations throughout.*

Molly saw Carmen put her phone in the caftan's pocket. Nick shifted the gun to his left hand but kept it near her temple.

"You do know, don't you…?" He drew a circle on her cheek with the pistol's muzzle. "If she shows up with police or even if the police show up by themselves, you're dead."

"Like Jasper?" she spat.

He grinned, but not in a friendly way. "You could say that."

He's admitting it, Molly thought. *He's going to kill me and Emma too when she gets here. I've got to call her back.*

Molly's eyes fixed on a row of red blooming hibiscus lining the fence on the left side of the house. They had been small when she'd first seen them five years ago. The other side along the driveway was divided from the house next to it by a tall hedge of Florida anise, holly, and wax myrtle.

Carmen rested with one foot on the Lincoln's bumper revealing a long, plump leg through the side slit in her caftan. The pose made her look sexy and tough. She said, "While we're waiting, let's go inside and do a line."

"First, why don't you call Philippe?" Nick said.

Carmen took her foot down. "Nick, I don't want to talk to him." Her voice sounded fearful.

"I said call him," Nick said, giving her a hard look.

"Oh, okay."

Carmen stepped into the back yard out of hearing range. In a couple of minutes, she came back and reported, "He's on his way."

Nick pulled Molly through the side door to Carmen's 1960's kitchen. Molly remembered Carmen trying to replace the wall oven—in turquoise, no less. From the looks of it, she had succeeded. *Time has moved on*, Molly thought. When she felt the nose of the gun against her spine, she felt ice all the way down each vertebra. *And my time may be about to end.*

Nick pushed her through the kitchen door into the living room and down onto the couch where Carmen was already sitting. He slumped down himself next to Molly. It was a tight squeeze. Her elbow bumped Carmen's, and she tried to move it. Carmen leaned forward to make a line in the pile of white powder on the coffee table. Molly stared. She had a hard time realizing just how much cocaine she and Carmen had snorted that week she'd stayed over. If anyone had told her that she'd be sitting next to Carmen again in front of a line of coke, she wouldn't have believed it.

"You want to go first, Molly?" Carmen held out a rolled-up dollar bill.

Molly shook her head. "No thanks."

"Oh, come on. Your girlfriend isn't here to judge you."

"I told you I've quit."

Carmen had one end of the dollar in her nose and with the other nostril held closed by her finger, the dollar's other end chased a bumpy line of cocaine across the mirror. When she finished, she sniffed deeply. She passed the mirror to Nick.

"Hold this for me," Nick said as he reached across Molly and handed the gun to Carmen. Molly thought briefly about knocking it out of his hand, but she was shaking too hard. Carmen handled it gingerly. *I couldn't have gotten far anyway,* Molly thought, *not with the hatchback parked bumper to bumper behind my van.*

"Gun," Nick said to Carmen after snorting.

She handed it to him with the handle out. "Keep it," Carmen said. "Guns make me nervous."

"As they should." Nick put the muzzle against Molly's temple again.

When is Emma going to get here? I should have called the cops in the first place instead of coming here by myself. If I had, I wouldn't be sitting right next to someone who probably killed Jasper and wouldn't hesitate to shoot me. After one murder, was it easier? What am I doing here? Did I really think that if I asked Carmen about the boxes and the lie she told about Manny, that Carmen would just blurt out what she knew?

"Where's your damn friend?" Nick demanded, elbowing Molly.

"I don't know. She should be here soon." Molly felt sick. *I've got to warn Emma.* But Carmen had her phone.

"Sure you don't want a snort, Molly?" Carmen held the mirror in front of her.

She hesitated. "I don't think so." She paused and spoke in what she hoped sounded like a soft and intimate voice. "Hey, Carmen, could we talk privately?"

Carmen said, "Actually, there's something I want to give you." She turned to Nick. "We're going to go into the other room. She can't go anywhere."

"You better make sure she doesn't try."

Molly let herself be led into Carmen's bedroom. She looked around. The old dressing table with a round mirror was still there. The king-sized bed still took up over half the room. An Oriental rug she hadn't seen before, in brilliant reds and blues, covered most of the tile floor. A couple of new pieces of art hung on the walls and a few framed prints leaned against the open closet door. Carmen must be doing well.

Carmen pulled the door to and stooped by a small safe by the bed. She spun the combination lock. She counted out three hundred dollars and handed it to Molly. "Look, I'm really sorry. You don't know how much I've beaten myself up over the money. I've literally kicked myself for letting it come between us."

Literally, huh, Molly thought. "This is too much. You took two fifty." She held out a fifty.

Carmen waved a hand. All of her fingernails were long except for the middle one. Molly wondered if Carmen had a girlfriend. "Forget about it. Just call it interest."

"Thanks, Carmen." *What a good will gesture, giving that money back, with interest, knowing I'm going to be killed soon!*

"What do you want to talk in private about?" Carmen asked, her voice soft. She sat on the bed and patted the mattress. When Molly sat down, she again smelled Carmen's cologne, jasmine and ylang-ylang.

"Please let me call Emma."

Carmen looked Molly in the eye. "It's too late. I can't save you or Emma. Even if I could, do you think they'd let me live? You two just wouldn't stop snooping. This is about more than illustrations or valuable books."

"Do you know what happened to those illustrations?"

Carmen shook her head and smiled a grim smile. "They're worthless now."

Molly thought, *worthless now, but in the future?*

"Jasper quit on us. The cut-up books were a warning to others."

"So other book sellers are drug dealers?"

"Not exactly. I can't say more." Carmen looked down.

"Jasper was killed because he wanted out?"

"Yes."

"But who? Nick?"

"It's not my story to tell. But it wasn't Nick."

Molly looked at the windows. They were jalousies with screens. At least they weren't the small jalousies. If she cranked the windows all the way out, could she fit through? And what about the screens? At least the screens opened from inside.

Molly put her hand on Carmen's. "Carmen, you have to help me. Let me call Emma."

"No." Her usually bold voice sounded thin. "I mean, I'd help you if I could, but what would happen to *me*?"

"You can't just let me and Emma be murdered! Please let me call her." She couldn't let Emma walk into their trap. *What would they do with us, our bodies, our vehicles?* "Carmen, look at me." Carmen raised her eyes, those large, deep, brown eyes ringed with kohl and heavily mascaraed lashes. "Let me at least keep Emma safe."

Carmen whispered, "You're more than friends, aren't you? You look at her the way you once looked at me."

Molly felt tears well up in her eyes and rapidly blinked.

"Okay," Carmen whispered. "But keep your voice down." She turned a radio to NPR's "All Things Considered."

Molly said, "My phone. You have it." She held out her hand.

Carmen put it in her hand, and, with shaking fingers, Molly called Emma.

"Hello, Molly?" She was so glad to hear Emma's voice.

"Emma, listen—"

"I'm so sorry, I got lost and I was confused between streets and avenues—"

"Don't come! They're going to kill us!"

"I'm almost there!"

"Call the police! And—Emma—" Her voice croaked, "I'm sorry." But only silence answered her.

Carmen hissed, eyes wide, "Don't call the police!"

"Emma! Emma? Damn! I lost the connection." She sent a text in all capital letters, "GO HOME. BE SAFE." She looked around the room. A corkboard with pictures tacked on to it hung above the bureau. She saw some pictures of Carmen with her family, a picture that was probably of her parents as young adults, and…she took in a sharp breath. A picture of Carmen sitting at a picnic table with Mignon— and Jasper! Not exactly dealers, Carmen had said. The other book dealers had to be mules like Jasper and Eileen. She tried to remember whose books had been defaced. Bob and Sharon, Lynda Duvall, Jerry, Grumpity, Kraken. Why was Mignon involved in stealing their books?

She tried to keep her voice light. "Oh, so you're with Mignon, now, huh?"

Carmen snorted. "You've got to be kidding! She's straight as a razor blade."

"What is her role in all of this?"

"You ask too many damn questions," Carmen muttered.

Molly looked out the window facing the street and put her hand over her heart, feeling it thump. *How many more beats does it have? I didn't even snort any coke and yet here I am like a caged animal, feeling my heartbeat.*

Carmen had taken up an emery board and was absorbed in filing her nails. Molly looked at her bent head, the upswept, thick, dark curls and tendrils hanging about her face. She felt a wave of sorrow wash over her, for Carmen or herself, she didn't know. She heard the rumble and sputter of a vehicle outside and looked up. A dusty, vintage pickup truck pulled to a stop at the curb.

The bedroom door flew open, and Molly turned to see Nick burst through, gun raised and pointed at her. "Come on!" he yelled, grabbing her arm. "You're coming with me."

Nick dragged Molly out of the room and through the front door, holding her in front of him, gun pointed at her head. She stumbled, and he muttered, "Come on, stupid bitch!" Molly tried to keep ahead of him, her breath coming in quick, panicked gasps. As they emerged onto the porch, she saw the driver of the pickup get out and come around the truck. He was an old man with long white hair and grizzly beard, wearing overalls. A woman emerged from the passenger side. Molly's eyes widened. It was Emma.

Chapter 29
Showdown

Robert Louis Stevenson. Kidnapped: Being the Memoirs of David Balfour in the Year 1751, *London: Cassell & Company, 1886. First edition. Green cloth with gilt lettering on spine. Black end papers. Fold-out color frontispiece map.*

As Emma got out of the pickup, she saw Nick from Ari's pushing Molly through the front door.

"Molly!" Emma called.

Molly yelled, "Emma! Get out of here!"

Emma realized Ty was beside her, his gun drawn. He said to Nick, "Drop that gun."

Nick pulled Molly in front of him like a shield. "Don't you come a step closer!" he yelled

Molly stomped on her captor's foot, and he dropped the gun. She kicked it away and ran.

Nick, grimacing in pain, started to reach for the gun.

Ty's soft voice said to Nick, "Don't pick that up!" He glanced at Emma. "Go get it."

The gun felt heavy in Emma's hands. A .45 automatic. Automatics had always looked much more impersonal and frightening to her. She'd rather shoot with her old .28, still in her shoulder bag, hanging against her chest. As she trained the .45 on Nick, she was aware that Molly was look-ing at her in disbelief.

Carmen burst through the front door, calling, "Molly!" She stopped short and froze at the sight of both Ty and Emma covering Nick with guns, turned, and ran back in-side. Emma could see her peering through the window.

Ty held his .38 easily, keeping the area under his level gaze. "What's goin' on here?" he asked. Out of the side of his mouth, he muttered to Emma, "Keep him covered."

"That van yours?" Ty directed the question at Molly.

"Ah—yes, it is," she said, voice shaking.

"Give Molly the keys to your car."

"You fuckin' old fart," he snarled at Ty. "You need to go back to yer old folks' home or wherever you hang out." He tossed his keys at Molly.

Molly caught the keys and headed toward the hatch-back, but froze as Nick's face broke into a smile. A motor roared and gravel flew as a yellow Jaguar convertible spun into the driveway, gleaming as though it were part of the sun, light reflecting off its chrome and hubcaps bright enough to make her squint. *This can't be good*, she thought, her heart in her throat.

A slender man of medium height, skin the color of pol-ished walnut, head shaven and shiny, stepped out of the Jag. He held an automatic as though it were part of him.

Mignon, blond hair tousled, slung herself out of the pas-senger side and came to stand close to the driver.

"You?!" Emma exclaimed to Mignon. *And that's the guy she was with at the restaurant.*

"Philippe Apollon," Ty said, keeping Philippe covered. "You're looking well. Haven't seen you since I put you away in ninety-six. Or was it two thousand two?"

"Both. I got out on technicalities," Philippe replied, still smiling. "I always do. Helps to have a good lawyer." His deep voice flowed with a lilting accent that whispered of

Caribbean islands. "Now drop it."

Ty let the gun fall from his fingers.

Philippe gave a slight nod toward Mignon, who whipped out a small handgun and pointed it at Emma.

"Drop your gun," said Mignon.

Emma dropped it, despair filling her. Across the street, someone stood in their yard holding a phone to their ear. *Oh god, I hope they're calling the police!* she thought.

Nick hobbled over and grabbed his gun from the ground.

Philippe looked at Nick. "Nick, why don't you continue with the plan we discussed?"

Nick whipped two pairs of plastic handcuffs from his pocket. "Stick out your hands."

Mignon muttered, "Get the keys to the van."

"Gimme the keys," Nick said to Molly.

Molly, hand shaking, extended the keys to Nick. He grabbed them, almost knocking her over.

Mignon trained the gun on them both as Nick cuffed them. "Okay, you two, get in the van." Nick herded Molly and Emma to the passenger side of the van. He pushed the button on the key fob and opened the passenger's side door. "Get in," he ordered Molly.

Molly climbed into the passenger seat.

Nick opened the sliding door, waved the gun at Emma, and said, "And you get in the back." When she hesitated, he barked, "Come on, move!"

Emma glared at Nick. "There's no room in the back! It's full of books."

"Do I gotta knock you out and throw you on top of them books, bitch?" He stepped toward her and raised the gun as though to hit her.

Emma flinched. She knew that you should not get in a vehicle when ordered to by someone who means you harm. It meant certain death. But she couldn't let Molly go by herself. She knew what to do. When Nick started driving, she would pull out her gun and make him stop the van.

The van was close to the dense, prickly hedge. Emma noticed a narrow gap where neighbors could go through. Then her pulse raced, someone was creeping along the other side of the hedge, inching towards the gap. She looked at Molly in the passenger seat. Emma wished she could touch her, but she felt Nick's gun poke her between the shoulder blades.

"Step along," he ordered.

How in blazes am I going to do this? She hastily stepped onto the running board and maneuvered herself into a small space behind the passenger seat. The cuffs pinched her wrists. She heard a familiar voice say, "Drop that gun and step away from them. Now."

The next few seconds blurred as Nick's arm came up to strike at the new person, who knocked Nick's gun to the ground and wrestled Nick away from the van and against the prickly hedge. "Ow!" Nick yelled as the other man efficiently twisted his wrist back. Emma slid out of the van, reached into her bag, got out her gun, and pointed it at the two struggling men. One of them looked up.

"Stewart?!" she gasped.

"A little help here," panted Stewart.

Emma raised the gun and brought it down on the back of Nick's head. He went down with an "Unhnnh!"

Philippe yelled, "Nick?" Mignon appeared around the back of the van. "What's going…"

Emma yelled at her, "Drop it!"

Mignon dropped her gun.

Emma heard something thud against the ground on the other side of the van.

Ty's voice drawled, "Okay, Philippe, you know better than to struggle."

Emma yelled at Mignon, "Turn around and walk."

When Mignon turned around, Emma pushed her gun between the other woman's shoulder blades.

On the other side of the van, Emma saw Philippe face down and Ty putting handcuffs on him. Mignon stood as though frozen while he handcuffed her too.

Emma raised her cuffed wrists. Ty whipped out a Swiss army knife and sliced off her cuffs.

Stewart, holding Nick by the arm, emerged from behind the van, followed by Molly.

Emma started to go to her, arms open, but then remembered she still had Nick's gun in her hand. She handed it to Ty.

He cut Molly's handcuffs off and took Nick's gun. "You all right?" he asked Molly.

"I think I'm okay."

Emma hugged her. They stood, arms around each other. Molly pulled away and looked Emma in the face, hands on either side of her head. "You're a badass," she said softly, "handling that gun like a pro."

Stewart cleared his throat.

"You're pretty amazing too, Stewart!" Molly said.

A siren sounded as a cop car careened around the corner.

The two uniformed officers came up, and Ty walked up to them. "I'm retired Detective Ty Olson. Those two," he said, pointing at Philippe and Nick, "Attempt to kidnap. Better check their guns." He glanced at Mignon. "Arrest her too."

A black Crown Vic pulled up next to the squad car, and Detectives Greenfield and Rodriguez got out. Rodriguez looked at Ty and went to the officers, who had subdued and cuffed Mignon. "Mignon Chambray?"

"Yes!" spat Mignon. "Why am I handcuffed?"

Rodriguez said, "Mignon Chambray, you're under arrest for the murder of Jasper Ross."

"What are you talking about?" Mignon's face went pale.

Detective Greenfield said, "You killed Jasper Ross in the parking lot of the Flying Dutchman."

"You can't prove anything!" She let out a sob as she was put into the unmarked car.

∽∾∽

After they had given their witness statements and the police had left, Carmen, who had been standing in the carport where she was questioned, slipped inside the house.

Emma said, "I can't believe Mignon killed Jasper."

Molly said, "I thought it was Nick or Philippe."

Carmen flew across the yard, her caftan billowing around her. She hugged Molly, whispered into her ear, and slipped something into her back jeans pocket. She gave her a long look and turned and walked back inside the house. Her thin caftan swayed around her statuesque figure. Emma watched Molly's eyes follow the tall woman as she walked away. *What was that all about?* she thought.

Molly looked from Stewart to Emma. "I'm so surprised at both of you for knowing how to handle guns! And, Stewart, you showed up with one."

Stewart scuffed some sand with his sneaker. "It's dangerous being trans, so I took some gun safety classes. I have a concealed carry permit."

"Good thing," Ty said. "I knew I could count on you."

Molly said to Ty. "We met last night, but Stewart didn't say you were a cop."

"Ex-cop," Ty corrected. "You can take the man out of the police force, but you can't take the police force out of the man." He scratched his beard. "Retired to work on my art, dabble in some art dealing, too."

"So that's how you and Stewart know each other," Emma said.

"You know," Stewart said, "I just came to St. Pete to eat

dinner."

A laugh burst out of Emma. "Let's eat. Nothing like being a hostage to whet the appetite."

Chapter 30
A Secret Revealed

Peter Christen Asbjørnsen and Jørgen I. Moe, eds., East of the Sun and West of the Moon: Old Tales from the North, *London: Hodder & Stoughton, 1914. Limited edition of 500 copies signed by the artist.* **Illustrated by Kay Nielsen.** *White vellum with gilt lettering and gilt decorative panel with blue border. Top edge gilt. In slipcase. Pictorial endpapers illustrated in black silhouettes and gold designs. With 25 tipped-in color illustrations, black and white drawings, and borders by Nielsen.*

Emma had a view of the Gulf from her seat on a wrap-around screen porch at Cecilia's Seafood. The sun wasn't near the horizon yet, but the sky was pink above the green water. The pier had three fishing boats all named after women—Sunny Sally, Belle Bonita, and Fishy Franny. Wives? Daughters? Emma thought back to the day she and Molly had walked on the beach before starting their investigation in Tarpon Springs. That was where Molly had spotted Nick from the book fair. Who knew that only days later he would be ready to kill both of them?

They ordered from a chalkboard sign reading "Ketch o'

the Day – Market Price." They each told their tale of what happened that evening. Everyone drank beer or soda and ate shrimp, grouper, mahi mahi, crab, and oysters accompanied by hushpuppies and mounds of coleslaw, all served family style. As Emma glanced around the table, she thought, *we are really like a family here, aren't we?* The thought made her smile. The sun was sinking lower, and the clouds were blue and orange.

"Let's go back to my place and get Emma's car, shall we?" Ty asked. "Maybe you'd like to see my collection and my paintings?"

Emma said, "I'd love that, but we really need to find a hotel. I already checked out of The Dutchman."

Ty grinned. "You know what? I have a little Airbnb cottage that I rent out. You two can stay for free. And it's got a jetted tub."

Emma looked at Molly, who nodded. "Ooh, a hot tub is just what I need." Emma sighed.

"Sounds great!" Molly said.

Once in the van, Emma asked, "So what was Carmen whispering to you? Sweet nothings?"

"Oh my god," Molly said, shoving her hand into her back jeans pocket. She pulled out a wad of bills. Frowning, she unfolded them. "What the…?"

Emma took the bills and counted the money. "Molly, there's four thousand twenty dollars here."

"Oh, shit," Molly said, grimacing. "She told me to hang on to it for a while and ran off before I could say no."

"She was giving it to you in case the cops come back with a search warrant." Emma said. "That little schemer! What will she do with the cocaine?"

Molly groaned. "Flush it. After getting high."

Ty led the way in his truck, followed by Molly and Emma in Molly's van, and Stewart brought up the rear in his SUV. By the time they reached Ty's place, it was completely dark. His driveway, overhung with palms and vines, wound out of sight. Ty turned in, and the others followed. After bumping along the shell-rock, rutted track, sea grape leaves brushing the top and windows of the van, Emma was glad to see a clearing and a two-story house beyond. She and Molly got out and followed Ty along a path around the side of the house. Ty's home probably dated from the 1920s, Craftsman style, with screened-in front porch, gables, overhanging tile roof, diamond-glazed casement windows, and built-on additions in the back. They walked up wide stone steps to the back porch. An automatic light came on.

Ty opened the back door and flipped on the wall switch. A kitchen emerged that looked as though it hadn't been updated in six decades, maybe more: deep sink with old fixtures, lots of wooden cabinets, a gas stove that could have been featured in a 1940s Good Housekeeping ad. A large, rectangular wooden table with unmatched chairs stood in the middle of the room. Faded, paint-spattered linoleum covered the floor. Antique posters and metal signs ornamented the wall: Coca-Cola, Seven-Up, Esso, Pure Oil, Sinclair with the dinosaur. Emma, glancing around, thought that Ty was like many collectors—stowed his finds in any available space.

"Welcome to my humble abode," Ty said, waving a hand. "Would you like to see my books?" At Emma's and Molly's eager nods, he led them through his dining and living rooms, turning on light fixtures and chandeliers. The rooms were full to bursting with antique and just old furniture, set among cabinets and bookshelves full of books. In the living room, Emma went straight to a barrister case with glass doors.

"May I open and look?" she asked Ty. At his breezy, "Sure!" she carefully raised the wood-framed glass door.

"I'll be in the next room if you have any questions," Ty

called.

Emma sucked in her breath. "All Golden Age of Illustration," she murmured. She took one out, careful not to tug at the endcap, already fraying. It was a first thus *Mother Goose*, the first with Rackham's illustrations. She slowly paged through the red volume, gazing at the illustrations. Then she began perusing the shelf carefully, fingers touching spines as though reading Braille. All at once, she froze. In the middle of the shelf was…

Emma said, voice breaking, "Molly, come here!"

"What is it?" Molly joined her friend.

Emma's hands shook, holding a cream vellum book with gold lettering. "My *East of the Sun*!" She carefully opened the front cover to reveal the title page with its signature by the artist. She tapped the page opposite, whispering, "See, this is mine: 296 of 500." Then she turned to the frontispiece: Kay Nielsen's exquisite illustration of the knight in the forest—icy-pale, fierce, and delicate, like an embodiment of the North itself.

"But how did Ty get it?"

"That's exactly what I'm going to find out." Emma gently tugged the book off the shelf, tucked it under her arm, and hastened off to the dining room, where Ty was holding forth to Stewart about his collection of Howard Pyle illustrated books.

"And I got four of his books from this antique dealer—"

"Ty, may I talk to you a minute?" Emma's voice shook with excitement.

"Sure." He put down the Pyle *Treasure Island* and came over to Emma.

"I just wanted to know where you got this." Emma held out the book.

Ty opened it to the title page. "Oh, yeah, I just acquired it. The 1914 limited edition with Kay Nielsen illustrations *and* signed twice by the illustrator—first below the line that tells which numbered copy it is, and second…"

"Where did you get it?" Emma asked, breathless.

"Ah, I bought…"

"It's my book!" she burst out. At Ty's surprised face, she added, "One of the books Jasper took from me at the book fair, the only one that I haven't had returned. I've gotten them all back—all but this one."

Ty's mouth fell open. "Jasper *took* it from you?"

"I mean—he said he was going to show it and four others of mine to Eileen to see if she agreed to buy them." Emma rocked up on her toes with impatience. "Only, as he walked around the Coliseum, he forgot and left four of them in people's booths. I got the others back and took them to Eileen. She bought them and wrote me a check. But this one was still missing."

Ty frowned. "I bought this book from Jasper last Friday." He stroked the vellum cover. "Mighta been the last book the poor guy ever sold."

"But he couldn't sell it to you!" Emma burst out. "He never *paid* me for it." She felt an urge to snatch the book out of his hands and restrained herself.

"I made an appointment to meet Jasper in the bar of the Flying Dutchman Friday afternoon to buy some books," Ty continued. "He called me that day and said he had some beautiful first editions, illustrated, nineteenth and early twentieth century, that he thought I'd be interested in. I didn't have time to go to the book fair, so we agreed to meet around four. He was so excited about this book in particular. Said he had just bought it. Well, o' course, I was interested, seeing that I collect Kay Nielsen. But when he got there, he only had one book, this one. I thought that was a little odd, but I was so excited to see this book, I didn't question it. I paid Jasper what he asked and took the book. But I heard on the news next morning that Jasper was dead. I was shocked. I mean, I may have been the last person to have seen him alive. I called the police and told them about our meeting." He frowned. "Eileen never paid you for this one?"

Emma shook her head.

Ty nodded. "My check hasn't been cashed. I just thought Eileen was too busy with all the turmoil around Jasper's death."

Stewart said, "I'll tell Aunt Eileen not to cash that check."

Ty said. "I paid Jasper twenty-five thousand, so I'll pay that to you."

Emma gulped. *I was going to sell it to Jasper for seventeen thousand.* Aloud she said to Stewart, "I'll give Eileen a check for a finder's fee."

Ty grinned. "So, we've settled that." He pressed the book to his chest. "I'm just glad to get another of ol' Kay's."

"Oh, that is great!" Molly turned to Emma. "So, you had a successful show after all."

Emma beamed. "I know. I'll miss seeing that book on my shelf. But I'll be glad to see the money in my bookselling account, so I can buy more books!"

"Spoken like a true bookseller!" Molly said.

"Want to see my studio?" Ty asked. He led them to a room off the kitchen. As she looked through the door, Emma gasped. The studio looked as though Kay Nielsen himself had been at work, only on paintings never seen in any of the books he had illustrated. Watercolors of princes and princesses, princes and princes, warriors and pages, and elemental beings in various stages of undress, draped in gorgeous rich fabrics. They pursued their erotic activities on beds, sleighs, and palace porches, in icy caves, and on rugged mountaintops. Their smooth flesh displayed all shades of human and inhuman possibility from deepest ebony to glowing gold to bluest of blue-white. All faces were stylized, all bodies elongated, muscular or delicate. Over all arched purple twilights, indigo blue noontimes, or velvety black night skies filled with stars.

"These are new!" Emma said.

"That's right," Ty said. "New work by a new artist, inspired by the great Kay Nielsen."

"But aren't these forgeries?" Molly blurted out.

Stewart said, "Not if they don't claim to be by any artist who ever existed."

Emma stared at him. Then realization dawned. "Gunnar Knut!" she exclaimed.

Ty smiled from ear to ear and made a courtly bow. "At your service."

"You knew!" Molly said to Stewart. "And you led me to believe—"

Stewart grinned. "I'm good at keeping secrets."

Chapter 31
What a Difference a Day Makes

Charles Kingsley, The Water Babies, *New York: Dodd, Mead, 1916. Illustrated by Jessie Willcox Smith. Green cloth with gilt lettering, pasted down illustration on front cover. Illustrated endpapers. Twelve color plates, including frontispiece, and decorative drawings throughout.*

Ty's Airbnb cottage was at the end of a path that wove through the lush overgrowth. A hammock hung between two Florida holly trees, and rocking chairs sat on a tiled patio. The tiles were various shades of greens and blues. Ty opened the door, and Molly saw that the jetted tub was in the middle of a large room with a long couch against the wall and two armchairs. A small kitchen was off to the side and the bedroom was nearly filled with a king-sized bed large enough for two to stretch out without touching.

"The couch opens to a bed that's more comfortable than most sofa beds," Ty said. He flipped a switch by the front door, and small twinkle lights came on in the patio area. "Well, night-night, you two. Breakfast is whenever you're ready. Just come in the kitchen, and I'll whip up something."

Back on the patio, Molly and Emma each gave him a hug. After he left, Molly asked, "Want to sit outside a minute?"

Emma smiled. "Sure. I'm exhausted from all that trauma today." She pulled the hammock toward herself, and Molly headed to a rocking chair. But Emma moved over and patted the netting beside her. "Come join me."

After Molly settled in next to Emma, they were silent. The twinkling lights flickered over Emma's hair, face, neck, and shoulders, causing her to be now in shadow, now visible. Molly thought that Emma looked like the Queen of the Fairies, taking her rest in a woodland glade, her tiny attendants keeping watch. *And I hope I'm not like Bottom, the clumsy ass,* she thought with a silent chuckle. She felt Emma's body lying all along her own, its heat rising and making her pulse race. Emma's scent—a breath of jasmine and rose, with an undertone of sweat—touched her nostrils. She willed herself to breathe slowly.

Emma turned toward Molly and took a deep breath. Their faces were inches apart. Molly cast her eyes away from Emma's, only to see the curve of breast escaping the neckline of Emma's tank top.

"Molly." Another breath. "Listen, when I thought we were headed for a certain death, I realized that I didn't want to die without . . . without, you know . . ."

Molly waited. She hoped.

"I've been pushing you away." Emma looked right into Molly's eyes. "And—I don't want to push you away anymore." She reached her hand and lightly touched Molly's cheek.

Molly kissed the tips of Emma's fingers.

The lights flickered on Emma's shoulder, arm, and breast—light, dark, light, dark.

Emma's hand went around the back of Molly's head. "I want—if you do—"

Molly leaned forward, and they kissed. And kissed some more. They pulled apart a little. Molly slid two fingers into the strap of Emma's tank top and drew it down to her upper arm, exposing her shoulder and the top slope of her breast. They kissed again, and Molly's hand went back to the tank top, running her finger along the neckline.

Emma pulled back.

Molly's insides plummeted. "Too much? Too fast?" she asked, dreading the answer.

"I want this, I really do," Emma said. "But . . ." She cleared her throat. "I'm kind of funky after all that's happened today. I'd like to take a bath. First."

Molly breathed a sigh of relief. "Of course. After all, cleanliness is next to sexiness."

Emma giggled. "Let's go get in the tub." She rolled out of the hammock and held out her hand.

Molly took it.

☙☙

After a tasty breakfast Friday morning, they spent the rest of the day combing the St. Pete-Tampa area for bookstores.

They stayed two additional nights at Ty's Airbnb. For lunch and supper each day they discovered new places to dine on patios. The nights were filled with getting to know each other's bodies and minds, and some of their histories and feelings as well. Staying awake late, making love in the bed and in the tub, relaxing in the hammock, they felt they had been transported to another world of unexpected, timeless pleasure.

"I never expected anything like this to happen," Emma murmured from the hammock where she lay, looking up at the stars.

"Anything like what?" Molly nudged her over and lay

close by her side, causing the hammock to sway.

"I thought I'd be on my own always." She shifted her weight and curled her damp body close against Molly's, equally damp. Both were fresh from the Jacuzzi. "I thought maybe I'd have a fling or two, but I was determined I'd never give anyone a chance to take over my life again."

"I don't want to take over your life." Molly's voice was low and soft.

A breeze raised light shivers on Emma's bare skin.

"I know. That's the glorious thing about you. You're so deliciously self-absorbed."

"Hey!" Molly said, mock offended. "I'm not self-absorbed, I'm just focused."

"That's right," Emma murmured, tracing her finger along Molly's body, between her breasts, down her tummy, ending in a dark, curly forest. "One of the things I love best about you."

"You're self-absorbed too."

"I know," Emma said complacently. "I still wonder, though…"

"Mmmm, wonder about what?" Molly's voice was muffled as her face was buried in Emma's neck.

"I just wonder how our lives will be different. About what will change?"

Molly said, "They'll be different, but we can decide how. Nothing is graven in stone."

"We each want to keep our separateness. Our independence. Our—"

"Solitude." Molly finished. "I think we each need solitude more than most people do."

"Yes," Emma said fervently. "Even though I love being with you."

"Don't you think we can keep our solitude and be together when we want to?"

"I hope so." Emma looked up at Molly's face in shadow.

She could feel Molly's gaze. "A friend of mind had a therapist who told her that she wasn't really in a relationship if she and her lover didn't live together."

"I don't think that therapist is right."

"I don't either."

Molly leaned forward, and Emma leaned to meet her. They kissed.

When they drew apart, Molly said, "We'll do a different way of being together."

⟐⟐⟐

On Sunday morning, they were up early (for Molly anyway), and after a send-off of fruit, toast, and coffee from Ty, they promised to visit again soon.

They drove as far as Valdosta and stayed at Molly's favorite hotel there, with its own Greek-Italian restaurant that had Emma looking suspiciously around corners for signs of connection to Ari's. She perused the menu word for word.

"No falafel here!" Molly teased her.

"And no book destroyers either, I hope!" Emma returned.

Around midday, Emma drove up to her little house surrounded with its now overgrown garden. Before unloading, she walked around the front yard, touching new blooms, shaking her head over overgrown flowers flopping into other plants' spaces. As soon as she started unpacking, putting things away, setting up her bookshelves and getting the books back on them, she once again felt absorbed into her own home and life. Emma felt both joy at being home and sadness at being apart from Molly.

Chapter 32
Returning

Eleanor Estes, Ginger Pye, New York: Harcourt, Brace and Co., 1951. First edition. Illustrated by Louis Slobodkin. Cover art by Arthur Howard. Yellow and blue cloth boards. With dust jacket. Black and white illustrations by the author throughout. Newbery Medal winner for 1952.

In June, Molly and Emma went back to St. Pete to testify at Mignon's trial. They traveled together this time in Molly's van with suitcases, not books, in the back. They stayed at the Flying Dutchman, in a room with one queen-size bed.

"Just think, we could have done this the last time!" Molly flopped down on the bed and reached for Emma. "How many nights were we here when we could've…?"

"Hindsight! Don't think I didn't want to." Emma slid down beside Molly and snuggled up to her.

Molly's arm tightened around Emma. "Not that we haven't been making up for lost time."

"First unpack," Emma murmured, and kissed Molly's nose. She rolled away, stood up, and swung her suitcase onto the luggage rack. Molly looked on as Emma unpacked and carefully put away her clothes, taking care to hang up her knit black cropped pants and long linen knit sand-colored cardigan. She would wear them with a tank top, airy scarf, and dressy sandals.

"It's not like we're going to be here long. We'll just go, tell our story and leave." Molly hung up a pair of linen trousers and a short-sleeved pale blue hemp top.

"I guess." Emma carried her toiletries into the bathroom and called out, "I'm going to take a shower. A quick one," she added.

⌘

Early next morning at the courthouse, Molly and Emma were sitting on a wooden bench outside the designated room.

"How do you feel?" Molly asked Emma, who was twisting her hands together.

"I'm nervous, of course. But I'm glad to see this done." She looked down.

Molly craned her neck around to see if anyone they knew was there. Just then, the bailiff came and asked them to follow her into the courtroom. They were led to seats behind the front row, where a group of men and one woman sat at desks talking to one another in low voices. Prosecutors, most likely. On the other side of the room, they saw two other lawyerish types conferring. Sitting between them was Mignon.

After both of them testified about finding Jasper and anything they noticed about Mignon's actions, they stayed in the courtroom. It was nearly four o'clock when Mignon was called to the stand.

Mignon rose and walked slowly to the front. She didn't look around but took her seat. She was wearing a prison jumpsuit, bright orange, but she still managed to make it look stylish. Must be the way she walked, a sort of dignified sashay. Her blond hair had darker roots now, but it still fell in careful waves to her shoulders. *Did she have access to a curling iron in jail?* Molly thought of Marlene Dietrich in *Witness for the Prosecution.*

The prosecutor asked her to state her name.

"Mignon Chambray."

"Do you operate a book business called 'Mignon Chambray, Bookseller'?"

"Yes, I do."

"Where were you around three to four on Friday, April 27?"

"After setting up my booth in the Coliseum, I returned to my hotel to shower and dress for the book fair opening."

"Your hotel being?"

"The Flying Dutchman."

"Did you see Jasper Ross in or outside the hotel?"

"No."

"Did you see Jasper Ross at any time that Friday evening?"

"No." Mignon shook her head firmly.

"Are you sure you did not see Jasper Ross in the parking lot of the hotel?"

"No, I did not."

"At what time did you drive back to the Coliseum?"

Mignon thought a moment. "The book fair began at 5:00. I left the hotel no later than 4:45 to get back, park, and be in my booth at 5:00 when the book fair opened."

Molly scrunched her toes. But *she wasn't back right at 5:00, because Emma said she arrived late.* She wondered whether the prosecution knew that.

"Ms. Chambray, how well did you know Jasper Ross?"

"He was a longtime book dealer. I knew him in that capacity."

"How long had you known him?"

"Since I started attending the St. Petersburg Book Fair.

Around 1998."

"Were you friends?"

"We were friendly, yes. I'm friendly with most of the other book dealers."

She's cool as a cucumber, Molly thought. She glanced at Emma, who rolled her eyes.

"When did your relationship become more than friendly?"

Ah-hah, Molly thought. *Here it comes.*

"I don't know what you mean." Mignon's eyes looked directly at the prosecutor.

"Weren't you and Jasper Ross having an affair?"

"No!" Mignon snapped. "That's ridiculous."

"Hadn't the two of you been meeting at the Flying Dutchman for years before the book fair began? As you had planned to do this past Friday? Only something interfered with your afternoon tryst, didn't it?"

"I didn't…no! We never did any such thing. Our relationship was that of colleagues."

The prosecutor pressed on. "Something prevented you from your usual meeting in your room on Friday afternoon. And that something was—that Jasper didn't want to do it anymore. He wanted to stop transporting drugs from Florida to Ohio, didn't he? And since you were in charge of keeping the mules in line—the book dealers who also transported drugs—it was your job to bring him back into the fold, by force if necessary. You tried your wiles on Jasper, but he wouldn't budge. So, you killed him."

Mignon burst out, "No! It wasn't like that."

"Wow!" Molly whispered to Emma. "She just admitted she did it."

The prosecutor stepped closer to the stand. "You acknowledge you killed Jasper Ross?"

"Oh, god." Mignon looked around the courtroom as though searching for something, anything, that would dial time back to the second before she had spoken last.

"Why did you kill him, Ms. Chambray?"

Mignon sat still, head down. Then she looked up and burst out, "I loved Jasper. Nobody understands that. He was the most amazing man I ever met. Erudite, funny, irreverent, a little crazy…" She wiped her eyes and gave a little laugh. "I loved him. It was business, yes, but I cared for him. And then when he came up to me and…" She sobbed. "I had just parked my car and gotten out when I saw him open the back door of the Dutchman's bar and walk out. Slowly, as though he wasn't sure where he was going. He looked up and saw me. In that moment, he didn't seem to recognize me. I went up to him and said, 'Hi, Jasper.' It took him a moment. He said, 'Oh, hi.' I started to put my arms around him, and he stepped back. I laughed and said, 'Don't you know me, Jasper? I know it's been a year, but I haven't changed that much.' Then he seemed to collect himself. His eyes lit up and he said, 'Mignon! What are you doing here?' I said, 'I'm waiting here for you.' He wrinkled up his forehead and said, 'Oh.' Then he looked a little shamefaced. 'I'm sorry, Dear. I just forgot for a moment.' He looked at me with a sad smile. 'How are you, Darling?'"

Mignon sobbed. The bailiff handed her a tissue. She wiped her eyes. "I felt devastated. I remembered what I was there for. I thought, what would be the difference if I just left him here? Just said goodbye and told Philippe we didn't have to worry about Jasper anymore. He was—gone. But I couldn't do that. Jasper could still let some information drop, say something to the wrong people, all unknowing. And I was afraid of what Philippe would do if I let Jasper go."

"What happened after he recognized you?"

She sniffed and sat up straight. "I went up to Jasper and put my arms around him. He relaxed and hugged me back.

We stood there for a moment. My little revolver was in my jacket pocket. I whispered, 'Goodbye, Jasper.' I slipped the gun out of my pocket, pressed it to his chest, and fired. He died instantly."

Not a sound could be heard in the courtroom.

Mignon continued, "I let him slip to the ground and pulled him over behind the dumpster. We were behind my car, so no one could see us. I left him there, went into the hotel, and got ready for the book fair. I was only a little late."

Murmurs rose around Molly and Emma as they stared at one another.

"Let's go," said Emma.

They slipped out of the courtroom. Outside, Molly said, "I can't believe she confessed."

"It didn't sound like she planned to."

"No."

Outside, in the humid parking lot, Molly said, "I still have one more thing to do."

"I know. Meet Carmen."

☙❧

Molly sat at an outside table sipping an iced caramel latte. She touched her bag with the package for Carmen. She had made it look like a book wrapped for mailing. She heard a familiar voice say, "Oh, there you are!"

She looked up to see Carmen picking her way between the tiny tables. She wore a yellow sundress that stopped above her knees, and her hair was piled on top of her head with a few tendrils encircling her face. She slid into the chair opposite Molly and set down her large tote. She leaned back and gazed at Molly with a long lazy smile. "You're looking great, Moll. Your new girlfriend must be good for you."

Molly thought, *I won't let her get to me. In any way.* "Glad you could meet me here."

"Of course." Carmen looked around. "Not exactly where I would have chosen, but whatever." Carmen waved at passing server. "I'd like an iced Chai, please, with soy." She turned back to Molly. "Why are we meeting here anyway? You could've come to the house."

"I didn't feel like going back there, not after what happened."

"Oh, I guess not."

"You guess not? After being kidnapped by a drug dealer who was threatening to kill us? And for all I knew had already murdered Jasper." Molly couldn't keep the exasperation out of her voice.

"Keep your voice down," Carmen whispered. "I didn't have anything to do with any murder and neither did Nick." She stirred the iced chai and took a sip. "You and your *friend* were poking around where you shouldn't have, totally out of your league. It was your own fault that you stumbled into a situation—"

"A situation?" Molly found her voice rising again and lowered it to a whisper. "Being held at gunpoint, being forced into my own van so some lowlife can dump my body somewhere? You call that just a *situation*?"

"Molly, I'm genuinely sorry all that happened. I had no idea how it was going to turn out. You just kept pushing, you wouldn't let it alone. You should have just let it be. Some things have nothing to do with you."

"Nothing to do with—" Carmen's lovely face held no understanding, no guilt, no awareness. Molly shook her head. "Just forget it," she said. She tipped back her glass and swallowed the rest of her latte. "So Mignon confessed to murdering Jasper."

Carmen's eyes widened. "Huh." She pushed her chai away. "I took a plea deal. They said I could be charged with accessory to kidnapping if I didn't cooperate. So, I did. I told them everything I knew. I ended up with a charge of possession."

"Carmen, why don't you get out of it?" Molly leaned forward. "Now would be the time."

"What would I do? Can you see me bagging groceries? I haven't had a real job in twenty years." Carmen blotted her mouth and put down her paper napkin. "You've got something for me, I believe?"

Molly reached into her tote bag and took out the book-shaped package. "Here's your book."

Carmen smiled and reached for it. "Thanks." She tucked the package into her tote.

"No problem." Molly waved for the check.

"How's business?"

"Not bad. I had a computer crash and lost some of my inventory listings, so I have to catalog those books all over again."

"What a pain!"

"How's Manny?"

"Good. Enjoying his new house."

"He really *did* move?"

"What?"

"Oh, never mind." Molly had no reason to challenge Carmen at this point. She was sticking to her story. She picked up Carmen's check. "I asked you to come here."

"Listen, Molly, I want to apologize for what happened between us, what was it, five years ago?"

"We had a fling! A wild weekend. Well, week."

"Not for me." Carmen's eyes held hers, dark and soulful. "I fell for you hard. I never dreamed you would just drive away, and it would be over."

Molly shook her head. "You know, it wasn't just the money. You stalked me to my mama's house!"

Carmen blushed. "That was kinda crazy, wasn't it? But

I just couldn't let you go like that. I had to see you again."

"Frankly, it was creepy," Molly burst out. "I mean, we'd said goodbye and we'd get together soon, before the next book fair. It was time. I wanted to distance myself from you."

Carmen bumped her fist against her head. "I'm so stupid sometimes." She looked into Molly's eyes again. "I guess there's no…"

"No," Molly said in a soft voice. "That week was long ago, and we've both changed. And I'm with Emma now." She grinned. "I enjoyed our time together, I can't lie."

"I'll take that." Carmen reached for Molly's hand and squeezed it.

The server brought Molly's card back, and she signed. They both stood up.

Carmen smiled. "Thanks, again, Mol. For everything."

"Sure, Carmen. Take care."

"I always do." Carmen brushed Molly's cheek with a kiss. She turned and walked away. Molly watched her until the brightly colored sundress disappeared around the corner.

Chapter 33
At Colorado Indigo

Margery Williams, The Velveteen Rabbit, *New York and London: George H. Doran and Heinemann, 1922. First edition, the only printing with original color lithographs by William Nicholson. (Later printings did not use lithography to produce Nicholson's drawings.) Pictorial paper boards and pictorial dust jacket. Color pictorial endpapers. Illustrated with four full-page and three double-page color lithographs.*

July in Atlanta is hot and beyond humid. At ten in the morning, Emma was regretting the bra she had pulled on when she got up. *Should have just put on a loose top*, she thought. Already too hot to go out and dig in the garden. Weeds were taking over. *Oh, well. This evening, get the trowel and clippers and get out there, work a little in the long dusk after sunset.* She checked the weather on her phone. *Rain tomorrow.*

But despite the humid air, Emma felt her usual exhilaration as she stretched out her legs to catch the heat. She loved hot weather, even when it made her sweat. She sat in her favorite porch rocker, face in shade, the rest of her soaking up the warmth that was driving out her blood's usual chill. Her oldest friend had called her a reptile. *Yep, just sunning on my rock.*

Breakfast was over, dishes washed. Now to enjoy a third cup of tea before going to price some new books and going online to look for estate sales. A delicate sound of wind chimes issued from her phone—Molly's ring. Emma quickly picked it up.

Molly's voice. "How's it going?"

Emma leaned back in the rocker. "I'm just sitting here sweltering with a cup of tea. Doesn't make sense, does it?"

"Listen, Stewart's in town for the Scott Antique Market. Wants to know if we'll meet him tonight for dinner."

"Sure! Where?"

"I suggested Colorado Indigo. You know, that place in Grant Park with the sidewalk seating? It's got all kinds of food and is dog-friendly."

"Sure," Emma said. She had been there once with Molly and enjoyed the burger and salad. The evening had been somewhat eventful when Blavatsky had gotten excited at the sight of three dachshunds promenading with their humans and charged after the little dogs, barking and dragging the table, to which she and Dimitri had been tethered, behind her. Dimitri, the calmer sibling, joined in with supportive barking and pulling, and Molly and Emma had had to rescue their food and drink, calm the dogs, and fasten both leashes to a rail nearby.

"Emma?" Molly's voice. "Sure Colorado's okay?"

"Oh, yes," Emma tried to sound reassuring. She knew she was answering an unspoken question: *is it okay to bring the dogs? Yes,* she thought with an inward smile, *it was.* "I know the dogs love it."

"Stewart's got some news."

"What is it?"

"We'll have to wait."

Emma saw Molly and Stewart sitting at a sidewalk table as she turned the corner. She felt an absurd joy at the sight of Molly, her short, tousled, light brown hair, her lanky jeans-clad legs stretching out onto the sidewalk, her blue button-down shirt that Emma knew matched the blue of her eyes. Molly's dogs lay peacefully next to a bowl of water, their leashes fastened to the iron railing in front of the restaurant. Emma stooped down to greet them, and their tails started thumping. Blavatsky barked a greeting while Dmitri nuzzled her hand. She petted them both and smiled at their enthusiasm. *Not everyone gets that excited to see me*, she thought.

"Hey, Stewart!" she said, holding out her arms.

"Emma!" Stewart stood and enveloped her in a gentle hug. She smelled his light soap fragrance—was it sandalwood? Stewart wore denim cutoffs and a light plaid short-sleeved shirt open to show a tank top with an American Library Association logo. Molly stood up and encircled Emma in her arms. They kissed. When they pulled apart, Molly's blue eyes crinkled in a mischievous smile. *If I had a tail, it would be wagging right now*, Emma thought.

"You look good," Molly said.

"Thanks," Emma answered. The white linen tunic over black capris had been a good choice after all. Her grey-streaked black hair had been recently cut and swung at chin length. She knew she looked good.

"We were waiting for you to get here before bringing y'all up to date about the case." Stewart cleared his throat. "You know Nick turned state's evidence and got a plea bargain. He's serving about two years for false imprisonment."

Emma took a swallow of her crisp white wine. "That's all?"

Stewart went on, "But they wanted to get Philippe, and Nick's evidence will help nail him. Philippe's first trial is next month. He's charged with conspiracy for kidnapping and murder in addition to numerous drug charges. Then he'll be tried in Federal court."

"That ought to put him away for a while." Emma muttered.

"Mignon hasn't been sentenced yet. I guess they're waiting to see how she cooperates in Philippe's trial." He patted Dmitri's head. "Will y'all be called as witnesses again?"

Molly nodded. "We've talked to the D.A.'s office. We'll both have to go to St. Pete again for the trial. I guess to testify about the kidnapping."

"Well, I don't envy you, but please come visit."

"Absolutely," Molly put in, taking a drink of her ale, a dark, locally brewed concoction called Thunder Over Stone Mountain.

"How's Eileen doing?" Emma took a sip of her wine.

"So far, she's okay. The other dealers are in jail waiting for trial for distributing illegal substances across state lines and RICO since they all conspired to commit the same crime. Aunt Eileen's lawyer is trying to keep her from going to trial, arguing that she didn't know anything about it, that Jasper did all the handling."

"Hmm." Emma thought it wasn't likely that Eileen didn't know. *Bet she was in the middle of it.*

"That's her story." Stewart shrugged. "But she told me plenty. Mignon recruited and organized everybody who lived in big cities. Jerry is from Nashville, and Jeff lives outside of Richmond. Bob and Sharon live in Chicago, Kraken lives in Brooklyn, and Lynda is from Atlanta. Can you believe Mignon is such a kingpin?"

Emma thought she could. That condescending smile, the sugar-sweet voice. She felt a wash of leftover anger pour over her. *Don't dwell on it,* she told herself. *Mignon's going to prison, after all.*

Stewart said, "I suspect Aunt Eileen cooperated with the police." He took a swallow of his beer. "I was so worried about her."

"Is she safe now, do you think?" Molly shot Stewart an anxious look.

He held up crossed fingers. "I hope so."

Thoughts of Eileen, living in fear, filled Emma's mind as she sat silently. What had probably seemed like easy money for so long had ended tragically.

The waiter appeared and asked for their orders. Molly and Emma each ordered a burger with a side salad. Stewart ordered a vegan burrito with guacamole and black beans and another brew.

Once the waiter brought their food, they focused for the next few minutes on condiments and salad dressings and then on first bites and sighs of appreciation.

Emma broke the silence. "What about Carmen?"

Stewart shook his head. "She wasn't arrested, and she didn't get called as a witness." He scooped up some runaway black beans with his fork.

Molly said, "You know I met her and returned her money."

"You did? When?" Stewart asked.

"When we went back to St. Pete last month."

Emma glanced at Molly, who covered her hand with her own.

Molly said, "She'll lie low for a while and then resume business as usual. Carmen will always survive."

They talked about books and the Scott Antique Market, where Stuart was already set up. Molly and Emma said they would come by Stewart's booth tomorrow.

Stewart leaned back in his chair. "You know, Gunnar Knut may be going out of business. Permanently."

"What?" Molly and Emma both exclaimed.

"Ty says he wants to focus on his original work. He's

done all he wants with the Gunnar Knut line. He says he's feeling constricted, trying to paint like someone else, even someone he made up. He wants to try and see what his own vision turns out to be."

"Well," Molly said. "I encourage him in that."

Stewart said, "I think he's a bit tired of erotica. He wants to try something more challenging."

"He's very talented," Emma said.

Stewart smiled. "You know, he's seventy-seven. He said to me the other day, 'Stewart, my boy, I feel I'm just starting out as an artist. All that Gunnar stuff, that was just warming up. My best work is ahead of me.'"

"He's amazing," Molly said.

"Yeah," Stewart said. "He's that rare human being who is not afraid to be free. Not afraid to change and become himself."

Emma caught Molly's eye. Molly gave her an almost imperceptible smile. Emma thought, *Stewart is not afraid to be free either. And I took a leap of faith with Molly.*

They all smiled at one another, clinked their glasses, and swallowed the last of their drinks as the streetlights came on above them in the lingering Atlanta dusk.

About the Authors

"Lily Charles" is the pen name of Libby Ware and Charlene Ball. They collaborate on the Molly and Emma Booksellers Series, bibliomysteries about two women booksellers who solve book-related mysteries. MURDER AT THE BOOK FAIR is the second in this series.

Libby Ware is the award-winning author of LUM: A NOVEL (SheWrites Press, 2015). She is the owner of Toadlily Books, an antiquarian book business. She is past president of the Georgia Antiquarian Booksellers Association (GABA); and is a member of the Antiquarian Booksellers Association of America (ABAA); the International League of Antiquarian Booksellers (ILAB); the Atlanta Writers Club; Sisters in Crime, and the Georgia Writers Association. She is a fellow of the Hambidge Center for Creative Arts and Sciences. Libby lives in Atlanta with her dog Grover. She is married to Charlene Ball, with whom she collaborates.

Charlene Ball is the author of the award-winning DARK LADY: A NOVEL OF EMILIA BASSANO LANIER (SheWrites Press, 2017). Charlene has a lifelong love of Renaissance literature and history. She has taught English and Women's Studies, and in 2009 she retired from the Institute for Women's, Gender, and Sexuality Studies at Georgia State University. She sells antiquarian books with her wife Libby Ware, specializing in children's books. She is a fellow of the Hambidge Center for Creative Arts and Sciences and a member of the Atlanta Writers Club, Sisters in Crime, and the Georgia Writers Association. She volunteers with her congregation, the First Existentialist Congregation of Atlanta, and with other organizations.

Libby and Charlene live about a mile from each other in Atlanta.

www.ingramcontent.com/pod-product-compliance
Lightning Source LLC
Chambersburg PA
CBHW030754190726
48285CB00003B/848